THE GINGERBREAD PUP

CAT BOWSER

Contents

DEDICATION

For my fur-child Ripley, an utter treat and privilege to share my life with for a glorious ten years. May your spirit be ever happy with the denizens of the North.

For my mother-in-law, Eva, whose support, love, and utter joy for the season remains infectious.

CHAPTER ONE

A more vibrant and joyful Christmas Day I had yet to see in the many centuries I had been given the pleasure of being Father Christmas.

By all accounts everything was perfect—-stockings filled, presents perfectly presented, the smell of treats a glorious aroma through every home.

And yet, the children weren't happy.

I took a sip of my hot apple spiced tea, setting the spoon gently on the saucer's edge. The sift whiff of cinnamon tickled the nose in just the right way while the ginger and sugar were a balm to the throat. After hours in the cold, it was a comfort to the body, if not to the mind.

Comforting my mind was my next task.

My children weren't happy.

Well, maybe it was not as dire as that. (Noelle tells me I make mountain ranges out of gopher holes.) The children were happy but not as happy as in previous years. They still held gratitude in their hearts...I felt it. All emotions Christmas wrought ran through my soul. The soft, soothing blanket of goodwill that drove out even the darkest chill.

There was happiness, a gratefulness but there lingered disappointment. And it was not disappointment in gifts—though one could be forgiven for thinking that.

I was not immune to the toxin of selfishness; I occasionally felt such a twinge—always came with the taste of dull licorice—but this was a different feeling. The aftermath of the last taste of hot cocoa. The last twang of sweet, the final wisp of marshmallow, the final embrace of milk. That was what I felt now—happiness tinged with fear and despair.

Not of the lethal kind but of the more important kind. An emotional, spiritual kind

I'd felt this before. The occasional visit of this I'd grown accustomed to, but there was so much of it this year.

Had I lost my touch? Was I misreading the children?

If this worsened...the magic of Christmas was fading, losing its potency.

My heart ached.

I was Father Christmas! Santa Claus, Père Noël and so many other names I had long since lost track. The Christmas season was my responsibility.

It had been my idea, my project, as asinine as it was, and if it was failing, the blame was mine to bear.

If my children were not happy...if their hearts were not full, I had failed.

Unrolled in front of me, my list spilled onto the floor. Each name pulled up a face, pulled up a letter, pulled up their joys, their wishes. The beautiful voices. All my helpers—those posed in malls, stores, and community centers—were conduits, a vessel through which all their words found me.

Some children were so shy, some so sure that I would know the perfect gift. And why did they have any reason to doubt me? I'd been doing just fine for over eight hundred years!

I thought I was rather adept at it—

"I think you missed a house."

My cup clanked, and the spoon flipped as I set it down off balance and bounced to the wooden floor, dribbling cinnamon as it went. With a low groan, I set the saucer on the nearby table and knelt, picking up the lost silverware.

"Missed a house?"

I was certainly not the most organized of chaps, despite many attempts to correct this. Literal millennia put into the project. But my memory was infallible and each house I visited was a friend, a favorite child (they were all my favorites) so the prospect I ...missed one.

Well, my stomach turned and given it had been handling hundreds of samples of sweets, some well prepared and some obvious first attempts, all night, that was quite a feat.

My time spell would have passed by now and with the first sun (sometimes before) the little ones would be up! Up to find nothing? To see the hope in their eyes shatter...

"What house?" I stood, scooting the chair back so abruptly it must have left skids amid the wood. Snatching my red coat from the back of the chair, I faced the voice.

I stopped mid-way through wrapping up my coat—left arm in, right arm not.

Noelle, my wife, approached but that wasn't what held my eye. It was the tiny creature in her arms.

Small little thing but hardly the smallest I'd ever seen. Tan colored with a small pink nose, triangle ears, and a long tail that wagged as I approached.

"A dog?" Reaching out, I gave a light scratch under the chin. The little thing closed its eyes and leaned back, a light rumble of satisfaction coursing through its body. "Where did you find it?"

"Her." Noelle corrected me. "In the back of your sleigh, where you save the eggnog and cider."

Some families liked to leave variations of gifts for me. While I appreciated all of them, my tongue had no tolerance for cider or eggnog. I brought those home for my wife, along with any gingerbread (that was by her request rather than my dislike). I had a special section of the sleigh, protected from the wind and shielded from ruckus where they sat.

And, apparently, I had brought home an unexpected treat.

"Then she was no gift." I looked at Noelle and smiled at the wrinkles that perfectly aligned with her deep dimples. "No gifts are kept back there. Too much of a risk of ruining them."

Noelle smiled, letting her fingers run over the pup's ginger fur. Her brown hair had turned white long ago, but that cheerful sparkle in her chocolate eyes had lost none of its power. She could still melt me with a look.

The same way she was gazing at the dog in her arms.

"Maybe I misspoke." I reached out and lifted her chin ever so slightly. Her eyes...those who knew were well aware that while I might do the job, it was Mother Christmas that made sure everything was in place.

Even as she stood silently in the small den, her bare feet making nary a sound of a mouse across the wooden planks, authority swept off her in waves. A tiny, petite woman, who barely reached my shoulder when on her tip toes, it was no secret that the whole project of Christmas would have died out long ago if she'd not been around to take the helm as the organizer.

Setting up the different stations, gaining favor from the elves to believe in such a mission, obtaining craftsmanship lessons from the dwarves, the gift of magic from the fairies, and some other mysteries that she kept close to her chest—all the result of Noelle Kringle.

My skill with children, my understanding of their hearts, my idea of spreading hope each season...it would have fallen apart without her.

My Christmas Star.

And the stars that lit up in her eyes with every tiny sound that dog made.

Perhaps this pup _was_ a gift.

"Maybe this pup is a present for you." I chuckled, low, and let my belly rumble. "Dogs have a knack for finding people who need them."

She clutched my hand and with a soft sight, deposited the pup into my arms, with that musical laugh I'd fallen for centuries ago. "Clever thing! Tucked in with that gingerbread...she knew exactly what she was doing."

I laughed, a deeper, jollier one as the dog settled her feet and gave my cheek a lick. "Perhaps she felt she belonged there! She has the coloring for it, little ginger pup."

The pup barked, a high-pitched, playful sound.

"And naming yourself as well, are we?" I rubbed her head, letting my fingers massage her ears. "A clever furry wonder you are! Very well! Ginger, it will be! And we'll see what purpose you bring with you."

She rewarded my wife and me with a lick each.

CHAPTER TWO

T he village spread out before me as I stopped and kicked the frost from my boots. Unlatching the snowshoes, I slung them up over my shoulder, keeping my other elbow bent.

A furry visitor had insisted on coming with me, but the snow would have swallowed her. If I were to try to trudge back in just my boots, I'd have been waddling up to my waist.

As spirited as this pup was, I doubt she was a swimmer, least of all in frozen water.

Noelle had knitted her a dark red sweater which she wore proudly but she would have nothing to do with the booties that came with them. So, while she insisted on coming with me—everywhere— it was done by pulling items out of my bag the moment I tried to leave her in my wife's warm study.

"Give up," Noelle had finally advised with a laugh. "A Daddy's girl always gets her way, it's a fact of the universe."

So, into my coat, our tiny canine went.

I rarely ventured out so soon after Christmas. Usually lacked the energy for it, to be frank. One reason we prepped such a huge meal (and yes, I do help—my gravy and potatoes are well-known requests in all corners of the North) was so no additional cooking or extensive cleanup was needed after the holiday! For just Noelle and me, it wasn't much but it was special, nonetheless.

My usual method was to relax and relish in a job well done for at least a week before diving back into work. If I didn't take any time off, I would burn out faster than cheap Christmas lights.

Except there was no relaxing. Not this time. As soon as I woke until night waned into predawn, I was sitting, pondering, clawing at my brain for answers. The names on my list were burned into my eyes.

Noelle finally yanked the list from me, shoved my coat into my hands, and said, "Mercy's sake, Nick, go outside! Walk the forest, visit your friends, count all the colors on the Northern Lights! Just do anything but sit here and stew! If the answer hasn't appeared now by force of will, they aren't going to. Stop. Thinking. About. It!"

Well, no arguing with the wife when she gets like that, so my furry companion and I were off!

"Here we are, little Ginger." Her tiny nose poked out. "Take a gander."

The Christmas villages I often saw displayed in homes definitely took their influence from the worker village. Lacking the magnificence to be sure but as close as human minds might imagine.

Yet, the human replicas contained something these didn't. The houses and shops served as stations, as temporary storage, for the toys and gifts as each of my helpers completed their part and then passed along to the next. But no one *lived* here.

The bright colors, the festival music, the...well, the life.

There was a magic there we had not touched. Not for a long time.

Elves got all the credit, but all manner of magical folk contributed to this Christmas project: dwarves, Fae (which meant brownies, pixies, fairies, and the like) the Doe-Folk—

Doe-Folk don't even get a mention in children's stories. I suspect few know they exist and they seem content to be mysterious. So long as they have wood to manipulate and carve into art, they've all they need.

The dwarves are reserved in the folk tales as villains or greedy folk—a far cry from the talented and generous culture who never failed to offer a warm drink and song by the fire coals.

Then there were the Fae—fairies, pixies, sprites, and brownies...do not believe the tales that paint them as malicious. Mischievous indeed but in the same way children are mischievous—out of the joy of life, curiosity over what boundaries they can conquer but with no malicious intent.

I wish the world saw them as I did but that's what made Christmas so special. Their works made their way into the hands of hundreds of children and while their names might not be known, their arts would be spoken about forever.

Elves for cloth work.

Dwarves for metal and stonework.

Fae for details.

Doe-folk for woodwork.

The Misses and I picked the miscellaneous and any sweet requests. And we selected what went where and on Christmas Eve I set out, spell for time distortion in hand, and the night of miracles happened.

How long had it been since I visited, well, any of my dearest partners, outside of new ideas for the upcoming Christmas?

Too long.

But my feet still remembered the way.

I made my way forward, Ginger still tucked tight into my coat. She didn't shiver and the wool of her sweater was soft on my skin. But her nose poked out into the cold and her ears never stopped moving, eternally curious.

Hanging lanterns, humming brightly with every color, set the paths of cobblestone alight, bathing each step with a light warmth. Not enough to dispel the cold, but enough to convey comfort. Like a thick quilt by the fire on a stormy evening.

Noelle had begun the tradition of relighting the lanterns when she saw the Fae using magic orbs to see as they dropped off their finished projects.

What a waste of their energy! She'd said and after a quick discussion with the dwarven leadership, the lanterns appeared lit the next eve.

Long ago, when Christmas had been newly born, they cast all kinds of colors, with a warmth unrivaled. Tiny little fireplaces.

But they had gone cold far too long ago. Our fires were a poor imitation, but some light was better than none. After all, it only took one candle to chase the dark away.

The clocking and clanking of metal on metal decorated the still air, even as far away as the mountains were. It was as if the wind felt inclined to report on the grand magic being done.

Dwarves working late, already in preparation for this year, filling the night with the clang of hammers and the smell of coal. Occasionally, the scent of heavy eggnog, rum-based wassail, and hearty stew drifted out from their workshop. Distilled by distance but nonetheless potent.

If I bothered to stop, the wind would carry the music of the elves, the sweet scent of the fairies and pixies, the light trot of the faun and Doe-folk. It had been so long since I had the opportunity to appreciate it.

Suddenly, with all the energy of a thousand children, Ginger began to bark. Her pleasant, "hello new friend" bark.

Lifting my eyes, I looked around. What had caught her eye? Was someone else out here, despite the cold?

Another bark. Deliberate and directed to the left. I turned, still holding Ginger tight to my chest.

"Jai!" I waved. "That *is* you, isn't it?"

Ginger's sharp ears and nose had caught the Fae leader before I did. I suspect if she hadn't alerted me, I'd have missed him entirely.

"Father Christmas," He drifted down, his boots crunching amid the crusty ground. "Odd to see you out so soon after your work."

I don't know if leadership for Fae is chosen, given by age, or determined by some other factor. I do know that Jai embodies it but not in any manner I can describe.

All Fae come in various colors and Jai's were green skin, violet eyes, and long black hair, well past his waist. He has no wings but that has never stopped him from flying (a similar magic gifted the reindeer their flight) and no matter what commotion was about, his hair remained still as if ironed to his back and shoulders.

But there's always an air about him, a sense of awe and responsibility. His clothes shifted with the northern lights and if he was one's first introduction to Fae, then everybody's strict father would be thought to be Fae.

But I owed it to him that I could do what I did.

"I admit, this Christmas was...off." Admitting it aloud was nasty as if I'd swallowed bad cookie batter. It turned my stomach. Not that denying it made it any better but saying it...almost like I was tempting fate.

I wanted to be wrong.

"Was it?" His voice was cold, the same as always. "How so?"

"The response was...lackluster." I settled on after a moment.

Jai's expression did not change.

"Why are you out here?" I asked.

"I could ask you the same. But I can surmise. You seem to have acquired a new friend." His dark eyes settled on Ginger, but she was not intimidated.

If I'd not had a good grip on her, I suspect she'd have flung herself forward and merely expected to be embraced.

"I have. She snuck aboard my sleigh and has attached herself to me and Noelle."

A flickering across his face. Faint, nearly invisible. "Any traces of earth with her?"

"Aside from the fact she is flesh and blood? No."

"...good."

He said nothing else, turned on his heels and in a flash of color was gone.

Ginger batted at my beard and I smiled, touched her nose with mine.

"He's a bit of a hard nose but you'll melt his heart soon enough."

Was a bit odd for Jai to be out and about, though. I don't think he knew *how* to have unstructured time. I suspect even his dreams have time limits and transitions.

But some things I am not included in, no matter how much I might wish otherwise. So, I tucked Ginger close again and continued my walk.

The night didn't help much. I could still feel the disappointment, the loss of happiness deep in my gut. Christmas was meant to be the season where dreams came true, when all things were possible.

Yet, here I was, with a bunch of children who knew even Santa had failed them.

Santa was not supposed to fail.

With a yip, Ginger clawed her way from my coat and with a bound was in the snow. It all but swallowed her.

But resilient as she was, that tiny head popped right back up, ears fully alert and her tiny nose pointed to the east with another yelping bark.

"What are you doing, you silly thing?" I scooped her back up, brushed her dry then followed her nose which, in addition to pointing, was now twitching.

And why not? The smells in the air would have charmed the devil.

"Of course."

One house, serving as the entrance to the village, was also a home. The only permanent one outside of Noelle's and mine.

A home made of ancient permafrost, woven holly, and amber tiles. Yet always an open door with a welcoming fire.

Even a new puppy understood that!

"Well, if it isn't Father Christmas himself." The cheery voice came with the smell of bread, sausage, and the clanking of dishes, caught amid a whiff of the cold wind.

Wrapped tight in blue velvet and white fur, the older woman climbed over the windowsill rather than take the long way through the door.

She loomed a good two heads higher than me (and a good one head higher than even the elves) with the build of a mountain. Some would even consider her to have giantess blood.

She always denied such things. *Just big bones!* She always insisted. But, as Mother Winter, she had her own secrets I wasn't privy to. At least not yet.

She has been here since time became a thing, probably longer. Back when the world was just seasons and survival.

By all accounts, I should have utilized her title Mother Winter as a show of respect if nothing else.

But she preferred I call her Ieva. So, call her Ieva, I did.

With a light cry of greeting, she enveloped me in a hug equal parts warm and cold.

I smiled, giving a light bow in greeting as she pulled away. "And a grand winter you've given us this year, Ieva. Much joy to the children, I can promise you."

"Children don't require much to be happy," she pulled away, gently clutching cheeks as she spoke. "At least when they're little. Once they start complicating things like adults—oh, is that a puppy?!"

She squealed, hands to her cheeks and for a moment I saw both the wisdom of eternity and the youth of joy simultaneously in her eyes. She knelt, with the enthusiasm of all my children when their eyes caught the first color of their filled stockings, to greet my newest companion.

"Ah, yes, it is." I gently pulled the dog from my coat and Ieva immediately had her engulfed in her robes. I doubt the pup felt even a whisper of cold. "She named herself Ginger."

"Well, aren't you the cleverest little thing!" The icicles that perpetually hung off her long dark hair rattled in the wind and Ginger took a bat at them. "Have to establish your authority early on, don't you?"

She stretched her hand through the nearby window into her kitchen—where all those wonderful smells were coming from. Plucking a triangle-shaped roll off the cooling tray furthest away from the window, she took a bite. Shaking her head, she chose a second one from the closer sheet and offered it to Ginger.

The pup quickly accepted her offering, in two bites, no less, and gave Ieva a lick for her efforts.

"Liked that, did you? A pup with good taste." She pulled a second, holding it out to me. "Fresh from the oven."

"You know my weaknesses." Taking it, I allowed a moment to relish the smell—warmth wrapped in the creaminess of butter, salty and rich pork, the slight bite from onions—-

Wait? Onions?

My eyes darted to little Ginger, currently enjoying a second roll.

Could dogs have onion? I was fairly sure they could not! What would happen? Could I wrangle some residual magic to slip down to earth for a vet—

No, no, I'd made a vow!

But my pup—

"I gave her one without the onions," Ieva rubbed Ginger's head as she spoke and set me with one of those warm eyes-only smiles. "I could see you starting to fret about it, but don't you worry. I know better than to endanger anyone dear to your heart. And you hold everyone dear."

My shoulders relaxed in a pile of released tension.

Just like a mother, I suppose, to know one's emotions without even a word spoken aloud. I took a bite of my treat, my tastebuds decided to throw a festival of their own and I decided I could not wait a moment more to get the rest of the roll in my mouth and before I knew it, a basket of them, neatly packaged in cloth sat in my hand.

Ieva shook her head but with the good-natured chuckling of a satisfied matriarch. "Every year, you can't resist trying my new-old recipes."

I flushed, red as my coat. "Perhaps but I mean no ill will with it!"

She gently parted my cheek before I could continue. "As it should be!"

I leaned back, clasped the belly for which I was so famous, and gave a jovial chuckle. "My stomach knows all and it can only keep learning by giving it new information. What culture's foods are you on now?"

"Latvia and the other Baltic lands this year." Taking a bite of a roll herself, Ieva laughed. "These are *speķrauši.*" She rolled her tongue as if she'd been speaking it her whole life.

But, given that she *was* Mother Winter and the Baltic states seemed to be ever involved in communication with her, maybe it was. Or at least a variation of it.

"Continuing your goal of sampling every human culture then, I see." I accepted the goblet she offered and the scent of mulled wine was unmistakable. "How far have you made it?" I asked as I tipped the liquid to tempt my tongue. Odd thing, mulled wine. It somehow managed to be cool and warm with spice all at once.

A hearty laugh to match my own. "Oh, my dear Nick! A different culture each season—each holiday—and I've only made a dent. For every one I try, another culture emerges. I dare say I may never catch up." She took a sip of her drink, closing her eyes a moment, savoring the taste with a satisfactory hum in her throat. "But I shall enjoy the challenge!"

She polished off her glass, setting it down on the inside windowpane, tucking her hands into her sleeves. A grand image she was—towering, frost amid her eyelashes and deep blue robes that put the darkest ice to shame. A deep age to her, all the wisdom of the universe in her eyes.

Even Father Christmas can feel young.

"Challenges are the spice of life." I meant that, too. Oh, the hoops and jumps creating this Christmas tradition of gifts had been! (Just for the record—the prospect of leaving coal for misbehavior was not my idea and I never engaged in it. I blame parents for starting that aspect.)

I only ever set out to show that good would reward good. That there was hope and wonderful things in the world. They did not always come easily, nor without sacrifice. But if one kept their head up and was willing to learn, to tackle what came, rewards were sweet.

After all, what kind of life was one without growth? Without challenge? Without triumphs?

An empty, bland one. Boring. Listless. Hopeless.

Not what I had in mind.

Ieva laughed as she sampled another of those glorious meat rolls. Rolls she'd only discovered because of her insatiable curiosity.

"If only more people took your approach, Ieva." I would have much preferred to exchange pleasantries until my nose froze. Then, I would protest as long as appropriate when she offered her famous cocoa.

Not as good as my wife's but quite close!

(Well...maybe a little better. By a minuscule margin. But we'll keep that difference a secret only for certain ears.)

Trading stories until we ran out of energy was tempting and was fully prepared to do just that!

But Ieva has little patience for beating around the bush—she'd likely be coarse and lecture about "wasting so much energy when a straightforward inquiry would do."

Except I didn't come here for advice. It wasn't proper to burden her with my troubles. I hadn't meant to even visit at all, beyond a mere 'hello.'

But I could tell by the sheen in her eyes that my attempts to pass time with distraction had been a failure.

"Well, let's not freeze out here! Much as I find it pleasant, I suspect you do not." She fluffed her robes, letting sparkles of white scatter to the ground. Tucking her loose hair back up into her hood, she closed the kitchen window's outer shudder as she made her way about the house.

She waved me to follow her inside, this time through the side doorway. Still clutching Ginger close to her chest, I could hear her chattering in multiple tongues (she tended to blend them when excited) and Ginger responded in kind with yelps and barks.

What they were conversing about was a mystery but if I were to wager a guess, I suspect my little puppy Princess was ratting out my fears. Tact is a foreign language to most children and it seemed this included puppy children as well.

As I stopped to shake off my boots at the door, her voice trailed back: "Leave your boots at the door, Nick. I know your feet could use defrosting. I'll even grab some of that cocoa you absolutely weren't going to ask about and we'll discuss what worries are absolutely *not* disrupting your sleep."

Maybe Ieva would have known even without my little canine spy.

After all, a mother knows.

CHAPTER THREE

G inger quickly claimed the small patch of green rug in front of the fireplace. Well, after she pulled one of the crocheted pillows from the wide cushioned chairs and rolled on her back enough times to wad up the fibers. Then, after curling into a "U-shape" with her belly to the flames, she slept.

Resting my feet upon the green fabric, relishing the warmth of both rest and fire, I accepted the warm mug of cocoa as Ieva settled in the chair opposite me, setting a plate of pretzels doused in frosting and chocolate on the table between us.

I sampled one—the contrast of salty and sweet was an odd one but always satisfying. The snap of the hardened dough, the sweet lick of the icing, the light crunch of the sprinkles. Fascinating what a glorious combination opposites can make.

She'd blessed me with her white cocoa this time. I believe Ieva has an endless supply of different chocolates and loves testing them out on me. Though, I'm hardly one to complain.

A swirl of cinnamon, the hint of nutmeg, melted marshmallow, with the white chocolate bringing them all together. The whipped cream and shaved ginger made for a lovely perk.

I think if Ieva was anything before Mother Winter, it had to be a chef because all her foods could be photographed as artwork.

"Now," she took a sip and wiped her mouth lightly with a napkin. "What's the issue, Nicholas?"

I cleared my throat and swallowed my sip of cocoa. "What makes you think—"

"Don't lie to me, young man. You're terrible at it. Why else would you come?"

"What?" I put a hand on my chest. "I'm hurt. Can I not visit my friends? It's the season for it, is it not?"

"You can. But you're exhausted, it hasn't even been a week since Christmas and your mind is somewhere else entirely. Ergo, something is wrong."

"Ieva, I--"

"Your hot chocolate hasn't drained one inch since we sat down and you didn't even notice the bowl of sweetened nuts."

I paused, looked down and sure enough, a large bowl full of peanuts, cashews, and all kinds of other legumes—each coated in a light caramel coating--was next to the pretzels and I hadn't even sampled one.

My sweet tooth was one of legend.

With a half downtrodden smile-that-wasn't-a-smile, I looked at her.

Crossing her arms, she leaned back, settling among the dark pillows. "Now, are we going to continue to act a fool or will you be honest with me?"

Well, if the centuries had taught me anything, it was to know when I was beaten. "It's the children. They aren't happy."

She raised a cynical brow at me.

"Well, not all of them are in any event." Clarification was important. "You know I feel when they wake up. When they're happy, it's like feeling it myself." I pressed my hand to my chest. The best part of my job. When all that joy, excitement, and thrill flooded my body, my heart swelled.

"It's not just their happiness, though." I took another sip, settling the mug on the table. "It's when they feel...validated."

Ieva hummed under her breath. "Oh?"

"Yes. Validated. They know that there's at least one person that listened to them." I closed my eyes for a moment. "Take Elsa. She babbled about being a great artist someday and capturing things, as they were, but "not the paints or crayons my parents give me." This morning, she opened her first camera kit and I felt her squeal here." I slapped my chest. "Or Aiden. That set of magic tricks will help him build up to being an entertainer."

Ieva just nodded.

"It used to be so simple. The children would write to me or tell me and a lot of them still do. But somehow, it's gotten around that Father Christmas is a mind reader. I'm not."

"So, why the change? Are you reading the children wrong?"

"Sometimes," I admitted. "The world grows every day, every second. I used to be able to visit each child, throughout the year. To get an idea, a snippet of time." I shook my head. Now? Even with the time-dilation spells I use to make my travels, I miss so many."

"So, you have to rely on what they say, what they write?"

"Exactly." I sighed and rubbed my temples a bit. "And some children...more than there used to be...cannot or will not tell me what's in their deepest hearts."

"What do they tell you?" She reached out and her hand clasped over mine.

"What they feel they can I suppose. Sometimes, I can infer what they aren't telling me. Other times, through the letters or what they tell me they despise." I winced. "That latter one though..."

"A risk." Ieva leaned back, nursing her mug, "I see your dilemma."

"Their lives are so much more complicated now. So are their desires—"

"Nick," Her voice soothed, rich chocolate poured over ice cream. "You know you can't and will not reach them all. Magically inclined as you are, a mortal man you remain."

"Mortal is up for debate—"

"Do not use sass with Mother Winter." Her veiled threat carried just enough bite to silence the tongue. "I mastered it when Rome was just an idea. You *know* what I mean."

"I do." Conceding, I leaned back, and let the soft cushions support my lower back. I rested my hands on my belly, and I'm sure defeat radiated off me. "I can only do so much."

"As it is, you half kill yourself every year. Look at you now." She shook her head. "These are the days you need to be resting, gathering your strength...you burn the oil through the night and wonder why your flame goes out."

Her glass made a tinkling sound as she set it back on the saucer. Reaching over, she let her fingers caress the little Ginger's ears as the pup snoozed by the fire. Her left ear twitched and she gave a low hum of contentment, deep in her belly.

Already taking after me. My Noelle was right—a Daddy's girl, through and through.

"But your heart has always been your best attribute, Nick. You wouldn't be here, otherwise. So, tell me, what is it—-truly—that sets your heart afire about this?"

My lips upturned, pulling pieces of my mustache as they went. "Are you giving me an excuse to talk about Yakima?"

A knowing shrug of the shoulders as she settled back in her chair. "If it applies, by all means."

I waited. When she didn't offer after a few minutes and the silence grew horrendously uncomfortable, I spoke again. "Borrow an icy wind?"

She blinked and gave me one of her whimsical, half-teasing smirks even as the cold of the season manifested about her pointer finger. A wisp of white and blue, all the chill of the deepest midnight snow, caught in her grasp.

She passed it to me and my skin tingled at the icy texture. After the initial shock, I cupped it, letting the magic of memory merge with the magic of the season.

"Can't do without your visual aids, can you?" The tease in her tone wasn't a lie but her words weren't either.

"I believe in what works." The wisp in front of me grew, growing both transparent as it spread but remaining translucent enough that only the features, not details, were visible. "Do you know how helpful it is when the kids include drawings?"

Invaluable. You would think requests for toys or treats would be straightforward, but you'd be surprised what "baby doll" or "book on planes" means to different children.

Icy white solidified, and a girl emerged from the wind—just as I remembered her. Long hair bound in a wrap, deep brown eyes, hands clutching a pail of water.

"Ah, that's Yakima, isn't it?" Ieva's voice soothed the air, the only thing keeping me anchored to the present.

"It is." She'd been my first child, the first one to receive a gift. Back before I knew of magic, before I knew I'd be doing this for centuries, back when I was just a lowly traveling craftsman who wanted to put a little joy into the world.

"I gave her an apple and a new pail." I laughed, relishing the remnants of her happiness that my memory clung to. "A simple little apple. She shared it with her brother. He didn't like apples, but he ate it anyway."

"And the pail?"

"I lost track of how many thank yous she gave me. Every day after that, I saw her carrying it on her shoulder, saying 'It was a gift.'" I sighed. "That's how it started Ieva. With a desire to make a difference."

A simple statement but all the weight of all the centuries was bound within it.

The wisp of wind dissolved, leaving a slight chill in the room. A snowflake landed on Ginger's nose and she awoke with a sneeze and shake of her head. Drooping her ears, she trotted over, pawing at me with a look reserved for only the most horrific of tyrants.

"Apologies, my little lady." Rubbing her head, I let my fingers massage her ears and chuckled as she leaned into it. "Oh, is that the spot?"

A half yelp as an alternative and when I pulled her into my lap, she stood on her hind legs, burying her face into my bushy beard.

"It seems that's still where it is, Nick." Gathering the empty plates as she spoke, she whisked out of the room in a flurry of skirts. But her booming voice still echoed. "But there's not the issue, is it?"

I stood, still cradling Ginger to my chest, and followed her into the kitchen. Seemed horribly rude to be calling across the room. "Believe me, if I knew the issue, I'd fix it."

"You're so young, Nick." She laughed but there was no malice in it. The type of laugh when amused and charmed. "You've grown in wisdom, but part of your strength is your ability to connect and stay so young at heart." she reached out and gently tugged on my beard. "But even that is fading. I remember when your beard was more brown than white."

She wasn't wrong. For centuries, I have kept my young appearance. But, somehow, it shifted over the years. Old age penetrated even with magic.

I used to consider it only natural but now...had that been when all this started? Had my own body been warning me all this time and I was too foolish to see it?

I frowned and watched her patter about the kitchen—from sink, to pantry, to stove, always cleaning, organizing, finding some nook here or cranny there which demanded attention. "Why did it change? Why did I change?"

She turned, wiped her hands on her skirts. "My dear Nicholas, the answer is in your heart and one doesn't find it because you already possess it. In a way, you already know it." A shake of the head then that knowing smile. "But the years are very good at covering it up, at dressing lace, frills, and silk over it so much that we do not recognize it anymore."

Looping her arm into mine, she patted Ginger on the head and then said, "Walk with me."

My pup leapt upward and landed with nary a sound in my arms. A light jostle of her head at Ieva, as if to say 'proceed.'

Tucking Ginger into my coat, I pulled on my boots and we ventured outside. The crisp, cold air caught our breath in puffs of steam and Ginger curled tight into my chest. A cuddly cloud of warmth settled next to my heart.

The snow crunched under our feet, the wind tickled my beard, and the soft moonlight colored the snow in blues and purples.

Beautiful.

"Look here, Nick."

Glancing up, a smile graced my lips. "A lovelier sight I don't think I'll see...at least until next year."

The pine tree towered over us, well over twelve feet tall. Every year, a special tree was selected and transplanted to the center of the village. For as much as the people on earth adored their decorations, there was little competition with the folk here.

Each group had their own days to decorate and they never intersected with one another. But you could be forgiven for thinking otherwise.

It flowed together so well.

Tinsel made of gold so think it was transparent. Garland woven from every flower in existence and dusted with silk shavings. Ornate carved globes of every size, colors as deep as the ocean, as bright as the reflection of snow. Slipped between the branches, encased in iron and glass, small lanterns gave off an otherworldly glow, an imitation of the comfort of a fireplace, yet not quite as bright.

Welcoming and reassuring, nonetheless.

And throughout it all, birds who had no means to travel, were nested, curled close to the burning lanterns.

"Over the centuries, humans have taken to coating the trees in all manner of finery. A reflection of their joy, their hopes." Ieva traced the nearby nettles, smiling as the gentle ringing of bells sounded. A sweet, light tune, like morning breaking the night with a kiss.

"But underneath it all, the pine tree remains the wonderful miracle it always was—-shelter, food, a source of inspiration, a fascination teeming with healing properties. Perhaps it's no wonder man chose it to be their winter symbol of hope. When their days are dreariest, the pine tree is where they turned."

See? There's something about hearing things from Ieva. I'd seen the traditions so synonymous with Christmas rise around the world. Not just the trees and wreaths but the dances, the different decorations, all the foods... but Ieva remembered a time before.

"So, you're saying my purpose has been...covered up?" Ginger poked her head out of my coat, sniffing at the tree, no doubt getting so many smells it would overwhelm me. "Is that the answer I've been searching for?"

"If I were simply to tell you, you would not understand it." I'm sure my face must have fallen.

Riddles. Non-answers. Was it asking so much for a direct reply?

"So...you do know?" I hoped the desperation I felt didn't reflect in my voice.

"I have...an inkling. But I surely don't know for certain because I am not you, Father Christmas."

I know my face betrayed me because she laughed that musical sound again and gently clasped my cheeks. "Do not fret so, my dear boy! Is this tree not just as beautiful when the decorations are gone? Do the tinsel, lights, and colors take away what it is?"

I shook my head. "No, I'd say it enhances what is already there."

"You're wise but sometimes even the wise need to revisit, remember, and re-center. Rekindle, revisit, and remember. All else will fall in step behind that."

She said it so simply as if she was just giving me directions to a sweet shop that deserved my parentage. Not a soul-searching quest to find my children's happiness.

"Where should I start?" I should have been embarrassed, maybe even frustrated. After all, one would think after multiple centuries, I ought to have an idea of how to tackle a problem, especially one so deeply personal.

But I'd come to Ieva lost so forgive me for my frustration at still being so!

She smiled, gently brushed the pine nettles and a light frost coated the green. Translucent, crisp, and leaving just enough green to bleed through. A decoration of her own.

She brushed my cheek again, leaving a light frost on the skin. And she smiled at me, hope painted all over her face. Her eyes sparkled as if she had all the joy of all the ages contained within her and could not restrain it.

It was a gift and she had to share it.

For a moment, just like in her home, it was as if I were a child again, and here was Mother to make everything right again. Despite having no more answers than I'd had before, I found myself full of optimism, bathed in hope.

"Where should you start?" Her warm voice sang. "I've always found the beginning to be the best spot."

CHAPTER FOUR

Pushing the plate away, I huffed, shaking my head. "Delicious as always, Noelle."

She scoffed and pranced over with her left hand planted on her hip. Lifting the plate, she pushed it under my face, as if it were evidence of a crime.

"Don't lie to me, Nick. You always eat more than this."

"But it wasn't a lie." I smiled at her. "The taste of the food is exquisite as always."

Pulling away, dishes clattered as Noelle dropped them in the sink before reappearing, without a fraction of time missing.

Or maybe I was so lost in thought that I never noticed.

"So, it's not my cooking. Not that I doubted it." She carried pride in her words, with good reason. I suspect even the most experienced of cooks could not match my Noelle's skill.

Having centuries to perfect what one was naturally talented at might be a pinch unfair, but the truth was the truth!

Slipping behind my chair, she wove her arms around me, kneeling to rest her chin on my shoulder. Even all these centuries later, her breath on my neck, her scent so close, that lovely voice coaxing my ear...I was a teenager all over again, with only eyes for her.

"So, what is it, Nick?" Her voice fell, clamoring to fix whatever had made my heart so downtrodden. I'd no doubt if the ability to mend a broken heart could be tangible, she'd have mastered it with voice alone.

As always, if there was anyone who could ground me, it was her. "The same as before."

"Still?" She squeezed me and lay a kiss on my cheek. "Nick, didn't you meet up with Mother Winter? She have any advice?"

"You told me to get some air. What makes you think I brought up my worries with Ieva?"

"Oh, I'm sure you hopped around like a rabbit, trying every which way to not talk about it. But I suspect she called you an idiot and pressed, resulting in some offered wisdom?"

It was a statement framed as a question.

I laughed without humor. "In a sense but I only have more questions. She speaks in riddles."

"Naturally, she's a spirit. I suspect you're regarded on earth with more than a little mystery."

A fair point. "Maybe but I wish the answers were clear-cut this time. Mystery is overrated."

She giggled, a young woman's laugh despite the age painted on her body. "And you'd say otherwise if a child had written to you about not knowing. You'd say that uncovering the mystery themselves builds character and resilience."

How did she do that? Somehow pick out a completely relevant moment and throw it back in my face. "So, you're saying to take my own advice?"

"C'mon Nick, I know Mother Winter must have given you a starting point. She's crafty but not heartless."

"She said start at the beginning."

Noelle stood, and shrugged her shoulders back, "So, let's do that."

"I have lots of 'beginnings,' Christmas Star. Which one do I start with?"

She smiled. "Well, let's work backward. When did you notice the beginning of the children not being happy?"

A good question. A pertinent question. I sat back, leaning a bit but kept my hands on the table. "I'd say five years ago. That's when I first started to see signs. I chalked it up to abnormalities here, an oddity there."

Had I lost my chance? What if I had jumped into it right—

"What brought it to your attention?" Her voice interrupted my thoughts and I thanked her silently for it. Take my own advice—

"I think it was..." Lots of things triggered my attention. "Well, I did notice the downward..."

I was fumbling. Tripping over my words. Not for any other reason than trying to solve a mystery as I spoke. My mind rushing and my mouth trying to keep up.

For all the good it did—

A low yelp pulled my attention down and Ginger's small head poked up, settling on my lap. Her tail swished back and forth as she gave my hand a flurry of dog kisses once she could reach it.

"A grand idea, little Ginger." Noelle grasped me with her hand, pulled upward, making me stand to greet her. Ginger leapt down and trotted after us.

It was to the wide window seat Noelle walked.

When we first made our home here, all our friends had worked together to make us a special place all our own.

The window seat had been the crowning piece: carved in intricate designs, with slivers of metals and brilliant red cushions. A true collaboration of all their skills, a physical manifestation of our agreed partnership.

The best part was the windows. I don't know, even after all this time, if they were enchanted or not but designs created of silver and white would form where we looked through them. They were translucent enough to notice but turned transparent whenever I desired to look behind them. There's magic even I don't understand.

Setting into the soft velvet, I pushed back, settling into the soft corner where the entire seat and wall contorted to my body. Magic inherent in handiwork was not unheard of.

Noelle settled next to me, reclining so her head rested against my belly. I adjusted my legs to give her more room. She curled close, burying her right cheek into my chest. I wrapped my arms around her, pulling her close and tight.

A light pressure settled behind me and a moment later, a furry blur leapt over us both, settling in the tiny section of space between the cushion and the window glass.

Ginger looked over her shoulder at us, gave a yawn far too big for a pup her size, and turned her gaze to look outside.

"Follow her lead," Noelle took hold of my hands, holding them tight in hers. "No answers come with you keep banging your head against the wall. Relax."

I sighed. "Noelle, if only it was that easy— "

"You're giving too much of your energy to this. Has fixating given you any answers?"

"As of now, no."

"Then stop baking an apple pie and being distressed when you don't get pecan." She looked up, dapped her fingers to her lips then tapped my nose. "Just enjoy the moment. We've had a full meal, the countryside is gorgeous, and you've got a beautiful wife and cute pup. Enjoy it."

Well, how did one argue with that kind of logic?

I settled and watched the snowflakes dance as they fell outside. The silver of the windows painted in patterns—trees, crystals, faces. Memories.

So many wonderful memories....

I smiled and gave a kiss to Noelle's neck. "Do you remember when we first moved into this cottage?"

"Like it was yesterday. The doe folk were so proud of it." She snuggled a bit closer and I relished her familiar scent of sugar, molasses, and pine. "Then the dwarves had to show off their work on the foundation."

"And who could blame them? When not even moving glaciers budge it, you have earned bragging rights.Just like the elves on the upholstery, the Fae on the flooring. The paneling." I looked up, held Noelle close, and allowed a breath of a smile. "True artistry if I've ever seen it."

My eyes traveled about the room—so much work was here. Intricate carvings of birds and animals. Individual panels painted in many hues. Different metals woven together until they danced in the candlelight.

They knew Noelle loved cardinals. Our kitchen, the reading nook, her dresser—covered head to toe in them. Bright ones, dull ones, dusted with sparkles and gems. It had been a one-off comment she'd said about how much she loved them, but my friends heard. They listened.

And look what came of it!

Centuries old, the craftsmanship looked brand new. Crisp, vibrant, sturdy, strong.

Work that endured. Work made with heart. "And after all this work, they were jumping at the chance to help me with my mission. I think you had to threaten— "

"Persuade." She corrected with a light jab to my stomach. "I persuaded."

"Very well. You persuaded them to rest." I shook my head, "And apparently resting meant drawing up blueprints, doing brainstorming meetings, and having at least five places set out for workshops before the next sunrise."

"They're just as stubborn as you." She reached out, giving Ginger a gentle scratch behind the ear. The pup leaned into it, a low rumble of contentness warming from her belly. "But maybe that's why you all came together so well."

"Perhaps..." I paused,hand halfway to pushing her hair back.

Ever had an epiphany? A realization that rings so hard through your head that your teeth rattled? One where you wanted to shake your younger self for not having the good sense to realize it?

Noelle shifted and looked upward at me. "Nick?"

"Maybe that's it." Saying it aloud solidified it, making it so elementary that I flushed red a bit in the cheeks at how simple it was. "Maybe that's where the answers are!"

Smiling, Noelle reached up, and caressed my cheek, twisting my beard around her finger, making me look down at her. Those deep eyes swallowed me and for a time, we were back amid the icy mountains of our homeland, leaving the expectations of our families behind for the candlelight that only burned when we were together.

"You found your starting point?"

I smiled and kissed her again. Slower this time. Relish her closeness, her scent, the way she wrapped her arms around my neck and painted the whole room with her smile.

"Thanks to you. How did you know talking about all those memories was the clue I needed?"

A soft shake of the head and the kind of laugh when she thinks I've stumbled about but still come out looking like I knew what I was doing. As if it had been purposeful. "Hard to find out where you're going if you don't know where you've been. And what clue did those memories unveil for you?"

"This started with friendship. The ways we bonded to all the others...so it's high time to rekindle that."

Rekindle, revisit, and remember.

"In the morning. After breakfast. You need to relax and if you don't pay attention to Ginger, I dare say she might take it by force."

A light padding on my arm. Looking down, if I wasn't greeted by the most obstinate scowl...

"In the morning it is then." I found the sweet spot, Ginger lounged on her back, showing off a belly of white and tan. "And yes, you can come."

Pounding on the door broke any sense of accomplishment. Sudden, sharp, like breaking of ice.

Noelle scooped Ginger up as I stood.

The pounding came again, somehow more urgent than before. When I pulled the door open, I found a dwarf, in mid-knock.

Eyes wide, hair and beard a mess, and the paleness of utter panic in the face.

"Father Christmas, the magic is dying."

CHAPTER FIVE

The children called it Gumdrop Mountain.

How they knew it resembled a gumdrop atop ice cream—wide, curling mounds of snow with protruding crevices of rock every color except brown and black—remained a mystery. I suspect that just as the magic I utilized seeped into the world, the imagination of children shaped the landscape here.

Would their discontent start to melt away the joyous sights here? Had it already begun to? The slopes seemed less dense than last year, and the snow less bright.

All signs. Signs I'd been fearful of. Any hopes I'd had that my concerns were limited to me alone fled with that simple knock.

What had begun with a plan to seek answers now had become a vital mission. Morning couldn't wait.

No matter how many times I had pushed Ginger into Noelle's arms so I could leave, somehow, she'd wound up twisted in my coat in my satchel, or between my boots.

Instead of frustration, I opted to trust. In what I don't know but there was a reason this pup was pushing to come and there was a reason she had ended up in my sleigh.

She'd altered me to Jai and I was entirely convinced that whatever had pulled him into the cold that night had something to do with this. She'd pushed me to Mother Winter.

I was not about to argue.

So, tucked into my satchel she went.

"Ol' Nicholas...what dragged you out our way?"

A split second later, my arms slammed hard to my side due to the vice grip engulfed all around me. Tight and fierce, even with my sweets-belly in the way.

But Father Christmas is never going to turn down a hug.

"Sapir, my old friend. It's been a while!"

How long had it been? The fact I couldn't even recall flooded my spirit, weighing down my bones. What kind of friend only called on matters of business?

And here I was again, here only out of need.

"Too long! I miss your horrible jokes." His rattling voice carried no sting, but it dug all the same.

My jokes...more like I was completely oblivious sometimes and Sapir, bless his soul, laughed it off. Oh, a nice conversation, a meal, and him nitpicking my metalwork would be paradise...

I hadn't done my own metalwork in years.

Sapir pulled away, gave a low slap to the arch of my back—the highest he could reach—and waved me to follow. No questions, just an invitation as if nothing were different.

But something was.

I could feel it, vibrating with each step, in the air, in the very way he held himself. The hidden-yet-not-so-hidden worry one doesn't wish to burden anyone with.

I was all too familiar with that weight.

Once we dipped into the dark of the mines beneath the earth, my feet clanking against the cart rails, Sapir took on a deep blue glow.

Like a blue-themed Christmas tree, giving off a deep, calming hue.

It was how I originally met the dwarves actually. I had been looking for a good place to set up my shop and literally fell down a hole (open mineshaft really but Sapir and I agreed that 'hole' sounded better). I stumbled around in the dark for a good hour before this gruff voice "Who's making the ruckus?!" came with that blue light.

That blue light had since then always meant friendship.

"We've been missing you, Nick."

I smiled, gently laying my hand on Sapir's shoulder so as not to lose my way. "Did you get my gifts?"

"'Course we did. You always leave us more than enough. And Noelle tells us *we* spoil our kids!"

I smiled and ducked underneath a gem ore creeping down from the ceiling. "It's hardly enough! Without you, there is no Christmas. Many things I am but a crafter and master of stone is not one."

"You are a worker of them. Perhaps not a master but you had the idea—hey! Dia! What are you doing here?"

The sudden sparkle of light red, almost pink, light exploded in the form of a female dwarf, hair bound in braided ponytails and dark blue eyes amid a pale face. Her arms burdened heavy with diamonds of all shades, she knocked Sapir aside, almost crushing my ribs in her embrace.

"I knew something extra bright was about! Papa Merry!"

That was a new one, but I smiled all the same.She was smaller, with less time woven into her grin. Her glow held less brilliance. Not a child perhaps but a young one.

"Get your foot off my neck, ya hooligan!"

I caught Dia as Sapir stood, grumbling and pinning his black hair back again. Some of his mutterings were in dwarven but one didn't need to know the language to get the gist. Words said in frustration were easy to decipher.

"Sorry!" Dia's apology was not ingenuine but was given in haste—the kind of haste when something much more important had claimed the mind. "But...you came! I knew someone came to alert you but...you came!" She clasped my forearms tight, tangible assertion of her statement.

"Well, I must admit, I wasn't expecting to be here today." I bowed my head. "At least, not until morning."

"You never sleep," Sapir grumbled as he forged ahead, keeping a grip on my wrist—though with Dia present, the dark of the tunnels had diminished.

"I do— "

"Not enough and you treat rest days as if they were a plague. It's not even been a fortnight since Christmas and here you are."

Grumpiness can mean affection; if judged correctly, Sapir always expressed worry with agitation. And I would return an insult—though not too harsh.

"You've some nerve, Sapir. Aren't you supposed to be resting as well?"

A low grumble, mixed with a snort and huff. "I am. I'm not in the forge."

Leaning over, I retorted. "And I'm not in the workshop."

It seemed selfish. Trading insults and pleasantries as if no one had rushed to my home in the dead of night, screeching about the miracles fading. About the power disappearing.

But I needed to pretend, if only for a moment, that what had started as a personal fear had not escalated into calamity.

A little self-denial helps keep you sane sometimes.

"But you're not here on pleasure either."

Shaking my head, I adjusted Ginger, made sure she was held tight, then said, "No. Please tell me what I heard wasn't true. About the magic."

"You're my friend, Nick. Don't ask me to lie."

It was chaos.

Workers running everywhere. Carts of gems, stones, and other materials nearly colliding with one another if not for the drivers' quick reflexes. Stacks of metal billets. Piles of raw metal ore.

And through it all, shouting in all kinds of dwarvish dialects, occasional items tossed about (I had to duck twice), and overall, the same kind of cacophony I associated with the week before Christmas.

But the mood was entirely different.

Coldness, fear, the unknown.

"Father Christmas!" A dwarf with deep green tresses bound in yellow gems approached and gave me a low bow. "Sapir, you brought help!"

"He's just here to— "

I didn't hear the rest because I was trotting to keep up with my new guest and that led me right into the heart of the noise. If I'd a century less patience, I'd have run the other way to rid myself of the future headache.

"I've Father Christmas!" My new friend announced me with all the fanfare of bringing home a celebrity. Or perhaps more accurately a surgeon in a war zone. "I've Father Christmas!"

"Father Christmas! Thank goodness!"

A flood of bodies, all colors and ages, swept around me, all simultaneously demanding my attention.

"Hold on!" Lifting my hands in surrender, I took a step back, almost tripping over a smaller dwarf behind. "One at a time."

"Sorry! Sorry!" Another chorus of voices. "We need your input!"

Four people said that, I am positive, though it was better than twenty.

Not much better but—

"One at a time." I hunched over; I hated to look down at people but if I got on my knees in this cave, it would take a century for my old bones to remember how to get up. "Why all the commotion?"

"Something's wrong with our crafting." A dwarf with copper skin and deep brown hair answered. I'm sure I'd seen him before but—

"They aren't enchanting like they should!" Another voice, feminine, from a silver-tinted girl with black braids swirling about her chin.

"They're breaking!" Another voice, deeper and matching the dark hues of his skin. "We've done nothing different!"

Breaking? Are their crafts falling? Impossible...

"The metal fails!" Another voice. "It crumbles in the children's hands but survives all our tests!"

"The clasps fail!"

"Look, look!"

I doubt I could have protested if I wanted to, but their words echoed so much of my own fears. It was not just my doubts. This...corrosion of spirit was spreading.

"See? Look! Do you see what we see? Father Christmas?"

The Seeing Pool. I had a smaller version of it—a snow globe formed from its waters and the ice of the mountain range. Whether the magic was in the water or the ice, I doubt I'll ever truly know.

But this was the raw source.

Wide as our cottage was long, with a deep blue color more reflective of the thick ice than cool snowflakes, the pool constantly ran. Ripples of current, a constant bubbling pool.

As I came to stop at its edge, the water stilled and took on a frosted appearance. Gradually, as fog cleared with the warmth of the sun, I saw my children.

To untrained eyes, there seemed no issue. But I saw the downtrodden gaze in their eyes. The slight dip of their shoulders.

And yes, the dwarves were right—the toys they had crafted did not hold the same majesty as when they were created.

The metal tarnished.

The Princess crown for little Josephine did not catch the candlelight and set the whole room awash in color.

The mini tool set failed to drive in the wooden plugs.

Little Maria smiled but the topaz in her bracelets had been emeralds when I dropped them off.

The blunt axe for Ryan to play hunter with was not meant to slip from his hand and slice his knee. It should not have even been possible.

All of these were checked and re-checked and checked again before they even left the mountain halls for the village storage.

They checked them again before they even got near my sleigh.

What was happening? First the children's emotions, then the gifts themselves? What was happening? Why was the magic of Christmas dying?

Why was my heart's greatest desire dying?

I had no answers. I didn't even have a cause.

But all eyes were on me to not just explain but to fix it.

"What is happening?"

"Why is this happening?"

"Is a darkness invading your sleigh?"

"It's Krampus, isn't it? He's broken our truce!"

"These are not reflections of our talents!"

"What do we do? What do we do?"

So many failures. So many voices. So many cries. So many questions. One after another, wave after wave. No answers. No solutions. No end.

To my knees, I sank. Staring into the water. And the images would not stop.

Child after child.

Broken toys.

Broken hearts.

Broken hopes.

My grip failed. My bag fumbled. Ginger spilled from my satchel with a surprised yelp. If anyone noticed her, they said nothing. I should have grabbed her up right away. But I was so fixated. On the failures.

My failures.

My project, my idea, my responsibility.

Ginger righted herself, strode forward, and batted the water. Just a paw here and a paw there. The water rippled, shimmered, and then turned solid, as real as a painting.

Jai. Jai from the night before. Or maybe earlier. It didn't matter when. What mattered was what I saw.

Other Fae, in a panic, just like the dwarves. Their own crafts failing. Their own magic failing. Any attempts to fix it, to repair it, falling as flat as ice.

Jai trying and failing to maintain the fear.

The fear that took his own eyes.

"It's happening with the Fae too?"

Slipping from the water as if afraid of it, Ginger pawed at me. Gently. Desperately. The room was awash in despair and I knew...knew from those round brown eyes that she felt all of it.

She wanted me to fix it.

"Our repairs act the same! Nothing works!"

"It doesn't enchant the children anymore!"

"It's everywhere! The elves sent messengers this morning!"

My eyes closed. I grasped at the ground, at anything solid. Anything real. Anything...trusted.

The elves? Had it spread that far? And if so, then what was to stop it? *How* could we stop it?

"If even Fae magic is broken, what do we do?"

Ginger hit my cheek with her paw.

"Did you see his face? Jai doesn't even know!"

"He always knows!"

"Father Christmas!"

"Papa Merry!"

"Nick!"

Scratch, scratch on my arm.

"What do we do?"

I snapped.

"I DON'T KNOW!"

My voice was not mine. It couldn't have been. How could something so cold and harsh be mine? I was the 'jolly ol' elf.' I was the spirit of the season embodied! My tone was meant to be cheery, to be the candlelight on a snowy night. To bring smiles and laughs. To light that flame of hope.

But you must have a spark for a flame and this was the final dousing over mine.

I should have known. I was supposed to know.I was supposed to fix it.

It was my job to fix it.

But I couldn't.

"I...don't have an answer." Lowering my face would have been easier than looking into those eyes—eyes looking to me for a solution. Looking to me to make it better, to make it right. "I don't know what happening, I don't know why it's happening."

"Is the magic dying?" A half-whispered voice, half crumbled as if afraid for the answer.

The same fear keeping my own nerves on fire.

"I don't know." Slumping, I slipped, my boots sliding into the edge of the pool. Frost broke at the edges and final swirls of color faded, leaving the reflection of the children for a heartbeat more.

A visage of the Fae burned into the ice.

I could see, just barely, outlines of the elves.

A whisper of the Doe Folk.

Whatever this curse was...it was everywhere.

The chilly surface permeated the quiet room. As wide as a room carved under a mountain could be, the silence created a chasm.

"This whole project was my idea." Voice parched and hard, it was like spitting pine needles. "The magic, the flow, the success...that falls on me."

I'd lost the power. Somehow. And despite my efforts, it wasn't being found.

And the children suffered for it.

"I should know. It's my responsibility to know. To know what broke." Broken. My voice broke. Just like all those spirits. Those gentle hearts that tried so hard to cover disappointment with a smile. Those crafts should have all but illuminated with the heart put into them. "I should know what we must fix. But I don't."

Silence. Painful, biting silence. The haunting howl of icy wind over a mountain. The emptiness when loved ones are gone, broken memories clinging to an old scarf.

The dying of a dream.

"I don't know what to do."

CHAPTER SIX

The reindeer grazed, back and forth beneath the trees heavy with snow. Occasionally, the wind would rustle, letting stray flakes drift down. It mingled amid their fur, scattered with each head shake.

There was a serene quality to the air, the land. A softness, a sense of calm. Easy to see why such a picture was used to represent the season on Earth so often.

Leaning against the naked tree, I reached out, rubbing the nose of the nearest deer. "Hey ol' Comet," I smiled. "Sorry to be intruding on your off days. I know you've got to be worn out."

He snorted, a gentle nudge against my hand but he made no move to depart my side. I took this as consent to keep talking.

"Odd thing, isn't it? Me not being jolly?"

A side-eye.

"Well, I mean outside of the frustration with so many airplanes and helicopters to avoid. And pigeons."

Pigeons were my least favorite bird. Hardly any sense in them. I was delayed at least four times a night by a stray one deciding to try and nest in my toy sacks.

"I didn't mean to snap. Truly I didn't," I reached up and gave a low scratch behind his ear. "Rather un-merry of me."

I didn't like yelling. I swore I'd never raise my voice. If I was to be Father Christmas, I was to illustrate the best of humanity, not the worst.

A snort warmed the back of my neck. I turned and Donder shook his head at me. (Yes, Donder. Donner was a misspoken name that stuck. He responds to both.)

Ginger shook and squirmed in my arms. I couldn't blame her. After the fiasco in the mountain, I was surprised she came back to me at all.

Like a slippery patch of ice, she popped loose and hit the snow, scampering toward the darker trees.

"Ginger!" My bones protested as I broke into a run after her. For such a little thing, she had significant speed! I suspect if she didn't have to jump each time because of the snow, I would have lost her entirely. "Ginger!"

I caught the barest glimpse of the tip of her tail, then a light airy laugh. Sliding to a stop, hands on my thoughts, I have a relieved sigh as one of the Doe Folk made their way out, Ginger gathered in her arms.

"Elder Noel, is this darling yours?"

Cloven hooves digging into the crusty ground, my visitor approached with all the grace of falling snowflakes. Snow white fur with faint black spots, a slender feminine upper body coated in the same color fur, large doe ears with curled antlers amid the sides of the head. Decorated with tinsel as we might wear ribbons, she looked much younger than I knew her to be.

Doe folk were, by nature, mysterious.

"Yes, thank you, good eve, my dear..." I trailed off, realized my words could be taken genuinely or as sarcasm, and slapped my face with a groan birthed in my soul. "I'm sorry."

"Why?" she settled, folding her four legs underneath her body. Her fur billowed, though only slightly, in the cold.

She had a thick shawl of woven wooden slats—fall colors- draped over her humanoid shoulders, but her fur was enough otherwise.

And all the while she spoke, her nose twitched and her large, coned ears caught every sound. Her eyes, brown and deep, took up almost half of her face and they never left mine.

She held Ginger out as if the pup were a peace offering.

The pup licked at the snow as it fell, oblivious to my faux pas.

But then, it seemed like my Doe Folk visitor was not particularly offended. Calm and still, she looked at me, occasionally tilting her head to the left or the right.

She was waiting for a response.

"I didn't mean to offend..." I paused when she shook her head back and forth. The small antlers that curled around her ears like living hair all but quivered with the movement.

I gently pulled Ginger from her hands, wrapping her tight in my coat.

"Elder Noel, you do not offend. I am part deer," she gently rubbed her back and smiled. "But you may call me Cerva."

She reached over again and Comet and Donder all but rushed to her side, called by silent music I couldn't hear. To each one, she smiled and brushed noses in greeting before turning back to me.

"The fact I share a kinship with the white doe and these wonderful creatures," she reached up and Comet nuzzled her hand, "is a blessing."

I sat there, quietly for a time. My visitor wasn't bothered at all, occupying her time with petting and speaking to the reindeer with their own tongue. An odd peace there was to it. For a time, I even forgot my troubles.

Ginger was content to curl into a ball, protected from the elements by my furry coat and large belly.

There was just us and the quiet.

"Isn't this better?" Her voice was gentle, freshly fallen snow in its tone. "We need not lose ourselves and twist our hearts into knots. A bunched muscle responds to warmth and rest, not repeated abuse."

Some wisdom in those words to be sure, though I wasn't sure necessarily how to

respond. Didn't seem right to agree when I appeared to be engaging in the opposite. Call me many things but a hypocrite.... "I don't usually see you or the others out here in the fields."

She smiled. "I think all of us heard the disheartening news from the dwarves. We've all seen reflections of it. I know our woodwork has never fractured as it has now." She let her ears droop. "I can only speak for myself but the splintering of my work I feel in my hooves."

Closing my eyes, I heaved a deep sigh—all the air in my body in one disappointing huff. "I know. I wish I knew what was happening or what we could do."

"Try listening."

What? Did she think I didn't? How dare—

"Listening? I always listen! It's vital to my mission!" My nostrils flared and I admit, the sharpness I despised re-entered my voice. How could it not with such an accusation? The visits, the letters, the correspondence from my helpers. If I did not know how to listen, Christmas would have failed long before now!

Ginger stirred, forcing me to drop my volume. I settled a hand in her fur, easing her back to peace.

"How do you listen?" Cerva did not even flick an ear at my defense and oh, if that did not rile my blood more! Did she think this was a silly game to me?

As for her question...how did I listen? By giving my attention and my focus. How else *could* one listen?

I voiced such. "Each letter, each visit, each little bit of information I receive is precious. It's a small window into my children's lives. With so many, I hardly get as much time as I'd like—"

"Do you listen to listen or to respond?" Her voice stayed soft, a mere whisper amid the wind.

And her question threw me off.

"Listen to listen?" I repeated.

She nodded. "It's a common ailment as years grant us experience and wisdom. We become fixers. All from a place of love." she reached over and lay her palm flat on my chest. "Your heart bears the pain of those you love. And you strive to alleviate that."

"Yes. If I can fix it or make it better. I wanted more joy in this world."

"But how can you truly help if you do not fully listen?"

Her hands moved, clasped my wrist gently, and I could not have looked away if I wanted to. Her eyes were unrelenting. "Before one is finished talking, you are planning your response. You are figuring out what you can do. Admirable but it means you miss so much of what they say. And don't say."

I stared at her. She spoke the truth, much as it pained me to admit it. I did try to fix things. Always have. But...at the expense of the person I was trying to help?

I grabbed her hand back. "You think...listening will provide the answers I need?"

She smiled with her ears twitching happily. "It has already begun, Elder Noel! Your heart is lighter having been out here! The quiet, the serenity has done its work. Do you not feel it?"

Pausing, I inhaled deep. Cool crispness flooded my lungs. Refreshing, cleansing. While my spirit was still heavy and my mind weighed down with worry, there was a peace, a calmness that kept my thoughts from overwhelming me.

My pup was content in my arms, such utter and complete trust in me.

I was in control. And I could tackle this.

"I do." Standing, I brushed the snow from my slacks, gathered Ginger into my left arm, and offered her a hand with my right.

And I smiled. The first *real* smile in days. The first time that spark of hope truly showed its light in days. "And may I say thank you for your wisdom, dear lady."

She shook herself off, her cloven hooves made a jingling sound amid the earth. "All I did was remind you of the knowledge you already had. It gets buried over time."

Buried. Much like a tree became covered in tinsel and color.

I had heard this before.

"All the same, I am grateful." I bowed my head. "How fortunate I am that you showed up."

She turned to head back for the deeper woods but glanced over her shoulder. "Oh, I may have been called."

Shifting my gaze over, I caught a distinct snort of satisfaction from Donder and a joyful stomp from Comet. As well as a laugh-that-was-not-a-laugh from Ginger. "And my gratitude to whatever...or whoever informed you I needed help."

Ginger yawned, far wider than necessary. As if to say, 'Not me, I had nothing to do with this.'

Even though she had, literally, led me right to Cerva.

"Is that not what friends do?" Cerva tossed her head to shake the snow from her antlers. "And what will you do now?"

I looked at her, and with all the passion I'd ever pushed into Christmas, answered.

"I'm going to practice listening to listen."

CHAPTER SEVEN

I t's an odd thing. Once something has been pointed out to you, the obviousness of it becomes so clear and loud that one ponders their own intelligence for missing it.

There is genuine effort involved in listening just to listen. I suppose at one point, many years ago, I was quite adept at it, but stumbling was the best way to describe my mastery now.

But the mere effort, the desire, the intent...it already made a difference.

How long had it been since I just sat, relaxed, and let the world speak to me? It had been so easy to lose myself in my work...

A low "yip" and tug on my pant leg pushed those thoughts away. Kneeling, allowing the chair to squeak under the movement, I smiled, wide and big.

"Oh, my apologies, Puppy Princess. Have I been neglecting you?"

Ginger tightened her teeth on the cuff of my pant leg with a *truly* ferocious growl and shook back and forth. Being so small, she couldn't shake her head without the rest of her body following suit. A tan tornado in a fur coat.

"Oh, we want to play now? Well, I suspect we can find something far better than my old pant leg."

Gently prying her teeth away, I straightened and slipped into the side workshop.

I didn't come here as often anymore. No reason to.It served more as a glamorized storage room than anything else.

But once, this was my magic shop.

"Ah, my little Ginger," I smiled as she wove between my legs, her nose twitching a mike s minute. "I'm sure you smell all kinds of things in here."

The old chair creaked when I grasped the back and turned it about. Loud scuffing along the wooden planks...I knew that sound so well.

Up and down, I used to be in this small shop. Putting together toys. Arranging clothes in boxes. Back when there were not as many children, when requests were simple. When elves, dwarves, and all my other friends would pass through, without any particular need in mind, and we would talk.

I'd be working on a toy, or they'd pick one from the pile and we'd talk. About...anything. Everything. The fireplace would be aglow and Noelle would bring fruits, cheeses, hot chocolate...eventually the fauns would start playing their music and no feet could resist that.

Now? Old benches that hadn't seen use in years. Boxes stacked high with old toys I'd never managed to fix. Bags of too many forgotten traditional toys that simply held no interest anymore.

But they were perfect for my pup.

Digging into the nearest one, I set aside dolls, old wind-up toys, and the occasional truck before pulling out a brightly colored ball.

"How's this, my little Ginger?"

Oh, onto her back legs she went, hopping about, front paws up.

"Oh, you don't want this, do you?" I jostled my wrist and the ball made a light, jingling sound.

She responded with enthusiasm. A low whine of anticipation broke between the last two barks.

With a toss, the ball rolled across the floor.

Like a bolt of lightning, she was on its tail, sliding a bit when she approached, grasped the ball, and turned back around. Back to me, she rushed, wrapping around my ankles before dropping the ball at my feet.

I threw it again.

Off she went, swift as the midnight wind.

Thus, our pattern began for a good half hour before exhaustion ran its course and she lay at my feet, panting but with the largest smile on her face.

Such a simple thing...just playing with a dear friend. Life truly was less complicated than we made it out to be. Sitting here, relishing in old times, did some good for my soul.

Oh, the toys I crafted here. The gifts I wrapped here. The bows, the special glitter, the double-checking to make sure I got a name exactly right. Seeing if I used red for Mary and green for Olivia.

My fingers ached. Oh, to do it this way again. To know every child as if they were my own...

"Ow!"

A sharp pain cut through my left foot. Not overly intense but enough to pull my attention down and out of nostalgia.

Laying across my toes was an old piece of wood, with a few flayed strings still attached. Age had done a number on its coloring but the moment I lifted it and caught the old carved initials, I swear it grew new under my touch.

Ginger sat there, head held high, pleased at the prize she'd found.

"My sister's old gusli! Where did you find this?" Cause there were tiny notches where her teeth did the pulling.

Ginger wagged her tail, tilted her head to the side, lifted her ears, and smiled at me.

I suspect it was under my old workbench, shoved in the back. Leave it to a tiny dog to pull out the oldest of memories.

Fingering the old wood, I dipped my fingers into the old strings. A light twang—out of tune—vibrated and I could almost see her. Hear her again.

"Nick! You got this for me? Where did you find it?"

Her eyes lit up, all the stars of the sky in those blues. With the strength of ten men, she clutched me, the wood of the instrument clunking against my back.

"Did some work for the carpenter. You need some kind of music to pair with your voice." I gently disentangled her arms from around my waist.

Her hands never left the gusli, holding the old harp as tight as possible. Her knuckles burned white. I hoped the carpenter's skill could withstand an enthusiastic little sister.

"How did you know I wanted a gusli?"

"You pretend-play one all the time. Think I don't see you hiding to listen to old Stacia by the square?"

"But how did you get this? I thought only old folk knew how to make one!"

I grinned. "I know what one looks like. Told the carpenter what I needed. And did work he didn't want to do for it."

"This must have been so much cleaning, wood cutting..." She ran her fingers over the strings, delicately and with reverence. "And the strings? That's not a carpenter's work."

"I have my ways. I'm glad you like it."

"Like it? I love it! Thank you, Nicky!"

"Now you can be that performer, Asha."

Warm fur under my free hand pulled me back. Ginger laid her head on my leg and angled her huge chocolate eyes up at me. Gently setting the instrument down, I stroked her head.

"Thank you for reminding me. I haven't thought about this for a long time. Yakima was my first child. But my first gift was this one. For Asha."

Ginger wagged her tail. Then barked twice.

"How did I get the strings?" Rubbing her head, I smiled. "I had a domra. I took three strings off it."

Onto her hind legs she went, and with a spring, she landed in my lap. A half yelp of inquiry.

"Oh, she didn't need to know. Would just have had a fit and felt bad. So that was my little secret. The carpenter made the body, I did the labor to pay for it and the strings were the final piece. Her gift was a group effort."

A lick to my nose and she nudged her head under my chin. A deep rumble from her, a deep warmth.

No words but I knew affirmation when I felt it.

A group project...

Lifting my eyes, they traced the ceiling. Where the Doe Folk had carved and Fae had painted. The way the glass and curtains complimented each other. The wooden planks, the chosen colors. The way metal, wood, and plaster interjected.

Like the strings, my labor, the carpenter's talent.

Different gifts, different arts...beautiful on their own, but amazing together!

"That's it. That's it!" Squeezing Ginger tight, I lay a kiss on her furry head. "You little genius!"

She cocked her head to one side as if to say "naturally, silly human."

"We've become so specialized...so separated. The magic here...my home is a group project! That's the secret. Christmas isn't just my project. It's all ours!"

I set her down gently and all but tore the door off the hinges. "Noelle! The others! Call the others"

"Which ones?"

"All of them!"

CHAPTER EIGHT

"**W**hy all the commotion?"

"You do know it's near midnight, right?"

"Ooo, Noelle is that cocoa? And cookies?"

"It's obviously about the fading magic!"

"Yours is dying too? I thought elves had eternal magic!"

"I thought dwarven magic was solid as stone."

"Don't see you rushing to help!"

"Hard to help when you don't know!"

I promise, it was not as hostile as their words sounded. Well, at least not quite as hostile. But if there was one thing I recognized straight away, it was the tone of frustration. Heard it myself far too much.

And when it was a combination of various people, of various races, well, there was bound to be some conflict. It had been a feat to get as large a gathering as I had: Kaiya of the elves, Sapir of the dwarves, Faluna of the Doe-folk, and from the Fae—Maia, Una, Reva, and Jai. Only Jai was not the diminutive size but that would hardly keep their voices small!

Jai, of them all, would not have missed even an inkling of magical discussion.

He, more than any other, was chilly at heart but this was important. Vital even. So, onward I pressed!

Standing up, I cleared my throat, but I had far too much faith if I expected that to gather attention.

Nice to get some use out of these buildings...it had been so long. Like coming home again. Nostalgia was strong.

But much as I loved dipping into memory, if I was going to make it happen again, I had to present my case.

Difficult to do if no one could hear you!

"Excuse me! Hey! I have some answers! We can work together! We can win Christmas back!"

Luckily, though when I told Noelle to call "everyone" she took me at my word. Including dear Mother Winter.

When my attempts at attention fell short (I'd never been one for calling attention, just handled it well), dear Ieva stood.

Remember, she has giantess blood (she might deny it but if you saw her loom over you, you'd argue with her too!) and it left her less than two inches from the ceiling.

With a voice that boomed like a winter storm on glass, she thundered: **"He said he wants some quiet!"**

Snow cracked in the air, showering down on the gathered group. Where there wasn't ice, there was water.

Kaiya rang out her hair and Faluna shook her antlers free of droplets amid Sapir's grumblings.

Pretty sure the Fae were the only ones laughing. At least until Ieva leveled a glare at them. A mother's glare had about as much power as a century of magic.

The silence was tangible.

With a smile and a gesture to the room reminiscent of a mother one hairbreadth away from breaking, Ieva said, "Much obliged. Please, proceed, Nicholas." Setting her skirts aside, she sat back down.

I stood, taking her place.

"I apologize for the late hour. I also beg your pardon for my...lack of interaction as of late. I have no one to blame but myself."

Kaiya stood. Her long dark hair, almost violet in the right light, held a few icicles from Mother Winter's outburst but her eyes burned with nothing but enthusiasm. "Father Christmas, why do you — "

"Forgive me but I do not deserve that title." Funny enough, I hadn't even thought about my titles until she said it. "It is not proper."

"Not proper?" The deep baritone of Jai, lingering along the walls, was not what I expected. If anyone was going to defend me, why him? "If anyone deserves it, it's you."

Shaking my head, I moved forward, pulling my chair to be part of the fumbled mess of seats currently serving our group.

"I didn't and I don't." Folding my hands on my belly, I smiled. "I won't say it isn't flattering. It's my favorite nickname. But that's why I called you all here. Well...partially."

Sapir took a swig of his ale, rubbing the foam out of his beard. "This about the magic? The crafts failing?"

From face to face, in each one, the mirrored fear I knew had dictated my heart since Christmas morning all but echoed. "It has been across all our trades, hasn't it?" I kept my voice calm as if talking to a shy child.

"It has," Kaiya answered. "Unprecedented. None of our remedies have any weight."

"Same with us. Just like you heard, Nick." Sapir shook his head. "Metals that could withstand the mountain falling on them fading, breaking, bending...it's not our skill."

"My people report the same." Faluna lifted her front left keg in sincerity. "Never before have our woodcrafts failed."

She patted the wooden designs hugging her shoulders. So thin they were translucent, yet they bent like leather. Wood made into liquid art. "Our own works are as strong as ever. But the samples we've made for the children...they chip, they break."

"Because we have lost our way!" My voice erupted but with excitement, with purpose. With solution! "Do you remember our first Christmas? When we all gathered here...before there were even buildings?"

Quiet. But the good kind. The kind where one contemplates. Where one reminisces and remembers. No words needed, no noise at all.

But I saw so much on each face. Memory is a powerful enchantment. Already, they were no longer here but centuries ago, on that sacred night.

The way Sapir sat back, leaned his chair to its back legs, and let his lips upturn, just enough.

The way Jai crossed his arms, looked at the ground, and let the light green glow illuminate his skin.

The flittering of Maia's wings as Reva and Una scattered amongst our tiny space. Emotion was not easily contained. They were back in that moment. That pinnacle time.

Warm hands rested on my shoulders and Noelle's sweet scent flooded my mind a second before her chin rested on my collarbone. For a moment, we stayed that way, relishing the memory ourselves.

"I remember it." She finally said. "We all were a lot younger then. Well, except for you crazy elves and fae."

Jai folded his arms behind his head., a light echo of a smile breaching his face, "I have no control over my bloodline, Mother Christmas."

"We don't either," Kaiya added as she took one of the few brownies left on the platter my Noelle had set amid the crowd. How it had survived the initial scramble I didn't know. "But we remember well. Mother Christmas had brown hair then. And you, Nick, had less of a belly."

"No need to insult him," Sapir grumbled. "If I recall, you hadn't grown into your ears yet and looked like a funny reindeer, darting about, wanting to help."

I laughed. "That's right! You were the elf child at our first meeting, weren't you, Kaiya?"

Her cheeks went light with color. "I was...intrigued by the concept. You were the first mortal to master magic and be accepted here. All others were repelled."

Noelle grinned. "I always thought you had some friends that let us in. Didn't Sapir introduce the idea of coming here?"

Snorting, the dwarf laughed in his throat. "He practically plowed me over runnin' here. Like he knew the way on his own."

Seemed like an eon ago... "It felt like I did. Well, and I never turn down a chance to sled in the snow. Blame the mountain."

"Thank the mountain." He amended with a tip of his glass. "She hasn't guided our hammers wrong before and she didn't then."

A light jingle and Maia landed in front of me, no doubt to be more involved. She was the smallest of the current fae and could be easily missed, despite best efforts.

Her red wings shimmered in the faint moonlight through the old windows. "I do remember. We thought the dwarves had lost their minds. Thought they'd jeopardized us all."

"Luckily," Jai gave a nod to me, which was saying something for the not affectionate fae. "While it is not in our nature to be wrong, it does happen occasionally."

"Anyway," Noelle interrupted before egos could fire, "As I was saying...that night. That first Christmas. Where the idea was born. We were right here. Before there were any buildings."

"Just tarps and blankets." The voice came from down by my feet.

Looking down, I chuckled.

Reva and Una came trotting out from the table on Ginger's back. While larger than Maia, they lacked her wings. But they had taken her example to move closer for conversation.

My pup was so proud to be a part of it. She should be! So much I owed her for bringing me to my senses, to the most obvious explanation. If she wished to parade about like royalty, let her.

Head held high, my pup crouched and leapt, landing on the tiny table just as Ieva removed the empty tray.

As full of magic as any Fae, Una or Reva could have changed their size at a whim. I'd seen them do it. I suspect Ginger had woven the same spell on them she had on me. They utilized her "offer" of a ride because she was impossible to refuse.

And that said a lot if one could charm a Fae!

Sitting as if she had finally been proclaimed empress after much toil, Ginger let her two riders disembark and lay on her belly. They chose to lean against her flank and Ginger did not protest.

Una spoke first.

Well, attempted to speak.

Her voice had always been soft and even with relative quiet obtained, the clanking of flatware, grumbles beaten conversations and the wind rattling the windows drowned her out.

She stomped her foot when no one could understand her, cast a volume spell in a flash of green light, and spoke again.

Her voice thundered. Full of power and hope.

"It was a broken camp. Food brought in shifts. If it weren't for all the magic gathered in one place, someone...probably you or Noelle—would have frozen to death. But the idea you had, Nick...."

Faluna picked up, pacing about as she was most comfortable doing, weaving between the chairs as she spoke, "It was the first sign of goodwill from men we'd seen in a long time. Far too long."

Silence reigned. Long enough to be awkward.

I forged ahead. So much bad history. So much justified anxiety. But...I could not let that rule tonight. Could not. Would not.

Fears be damned.

"I know. The faith you put in me that night...I don't know if anyone...except maybe Noelle, has ever trusted me that much. Especially since only Sapir knew me."

A light muttering, but of the good kind, scattered among the group. Taking advantage, I pressed on.

"We made a pact that night. Let's see what happens when we reward good. Let's see what happens when we put some joy, some magic into the world." I paused, waited for a time, then continued. "I know that asked a lot of you all."

Kaiya inhaled, and closed her eyes a moment before she answered, "I was not as privy to things as my elders— "

"A fault of them, not you." Jai interrupted. "But if I could be so bold, Nicholas, I doubt you have brought us here to reminisce."

Blunt and direct but what else do you expect from someone alive for centuries? Mother Winter was the same.

"No. I brought you here because I think I have stumbled on a solution."

"You've figured out why the gifts are failing?" Reva exploded to full size in a rush of red light, fast enough that it took her clothing a moment to follow.

I covered my eyes until I heard her curse and the light reprimand from Jai about not losing herself in emotion 'or your magic will frazzle.'

Her response I couldn't catch—rapid fae language but I could reason its general meaning.

Poor thing. Magic was hard enough to manage without a crowd of strangers. My first night as Santa had secrets I would take to my grave, whenever Death remembered me.

Noelle alerted me that "she's proper again, darling," and I reopened my eyes.

Reva's whole body burned with magic—a physical manifestation of her emotions she was trying (and failing) to reign in.

I smiled, "I'm glad to see you're as excited about this as I am! But yes, I think I have stumbled upon a solution."

Ginger barked twice.

"With some help from our newest member, naturally," I added as I gently rubbed the dog's head. She gave a low grunt of acceptance and went quiet.

"But bringing up our first Christmas was important." I turned my attention back to our small gathering. "We were so passionate then. For a long time after. But with time, we became...distant. All of us. Including me." I pulled my beard, "Lots of signs. Rationalized them all."

A failure. A failure I would never forgive myself for. If not for Sapir, Dia, Cerva, my little Ginger, and Mother Winter Ieva, well, I suspect I would have still been rationalizing it.

"But now...well, I'm a bit baffled how it wasn't so clear to me. When we first started this project, we knew the children. The magical helpers you all sent to earth would give me such information. Or the letters came so many times, with so much detail. Each gift was personalized. Each gift was unique."

"You were using your memory magic, weren't you?" Jai asked.

Stopping abruptly, I considered. Had I been? I didn't recall utilizing it but with so much discussion and knowledge of the children as the gifts were crafted...

"I think we all did, to some degree. Hard not to when you have so much of the child in mind as you work. Emotion fuels magic, doesn't it?"

Reva answered, her eyes afire with such truth it resounded through every fiber of her being. "As naturally as air fuels life."

"We've lost the connection." On this, I was most adamant. "I can't believe it's taken me so long to realize it but it's clear now. The little information we have is not enough. We must...know the children again."

"That fell away by need of necessity." Kaiya was intrigued though. Her eyes, the way they brightened and sparkled, were signs her mind was already beginning to work. "There were too few of us, too few of you, and too many children."

"With too many demands." Jai's voice clouded, tinted with grievance. "Even the good ones expect far more than ever."

I could not argue that. But, what if...

"But if the offerings they received were personalized, special, something uniquely theirs..."

"Then, a few gifts seem like so much more," Mother Winter clapped her hands lightly, pride evident in her eyes.

Clapping my hands myself for emphasis, I directed a finger at her. "Exactly."

Turning to the gathered group. "Here's what I'm proposing." I took a breath. It was a risky proposal. Especially given the history of some of my friends. The mortal world had not exactly been kind to them. But they had supported me so far... "I'm going to need help. Far more than we have now. But we have the numbers for it."

"Get to the point, Nick." Sapir leaned back. "You're stalling."

"We need to go back to how we used to do it—together. Collaborative. Not just one group finishes one part and then another does theirs. They need to be done together. The magic I've seen each of your kind do is a thousandfold when combined."

Noelle sat next to me, settled on the arm of my chair. "Our very home is proof of it. That is easily the most gorgeous thing ever created here. And it's because it was done together."

Quiet again then Una asked, "How do you propose we handle the memory magic? That is a core reason your cottage has lost none of its splendor and the gifts have."

Here it was. The breaking point. The one piece that might pull everything down. "We need to get to know the children. We can't just assign one family to one group. Spread out, that way the memory magic can manifest in every aspect of the process, not just one."

"And how do you propose we get to know the children?" Jai's voice was taut, pulled tight as a string, and cold as a blizzard.

I plowed forward.

"By listening. I owe it to Faluna's people for pointing out that flaw of mine. I was listening to respond, to gain information. We need to listen to listen again. Not just reports here and there. We need...connections with these children."

I took a breath and plowed forward.

"We need...all of us...anyone who touches the process, we need to venture to earth and learn about these children. Learn their joys, their sorrows, their goals, their barriers, their loves, their hates. The whole child. All we see now is reflection, a ripple in the water. You cannot paint a masterpiece from that."

"Go to earth? Not even you venture to earth!" Reva turned deep violet though I don't know if it was excitement or rage.

"No. I made a promise a long time ago. Take on the same exile as you all if I were to accept the use of your magic. Only to complete my mission would I leave here. No detours. No unexpected trips. I accepted your terms." I looked around. "I'm not asking to break those terms. I've asking to end the exile."

"With safeties in place," Noelle chimed in. "We aren't asking you all to flood to earth again. Not like that. Glamours. Disguises. Ways to be there...yet not be there."

"We've been here, apart from the world, for centuries." Kaiya pulled at her hair, twisting it about her finger.

"I know. And I know you had good reason to— "

"Nicholas!" Ah, there was the explosion from Jai I was waiting for. "You know not what you ask! It's asinine. Best to just scrap the whole idea if that is supposed to be your solution! We cannot! We will not!"

"Hey!" Sapir sat upright. "Don't speak for the rest of us."

"Indeed." Faluna crossed her back legs and set Jai with a harsh look. "Father Christmas has a lot of good points."

"And let's be honest," Kaiya added. "Something has to change."

"Not that!" Jai snapped. "You're too young to remember— "

"And things have changed!" Una interrupted. "Things always change. We should at least consider this— "

"No, I— "

I held up my hand. "Wait." When quiet followed, I stood and offered a hand to Jai. "Jai, walk with me?"

Oh, the dark glare he leveled at me. Centuries of loathing in a stare.

"I know this is important to you." I crossed the room, slowly but steadily. "But I'm asking you to consider...have I ever done anything with malice toward you or the people here? Will you at least grant me a few minutes of your time so we might each listen and truly hear each other?"

He eyed my outstretched hand like it was poison. But his own people were giving nods. In desperation, his teeth clinched, his eyes fell on Reva.

"Don't let emotion frazzle you." She said, simply. Building on the warning he'd given her earlier. No cruelty in her voice, merely an urging.

A plea.

Pushing off the wall with a sigh, Jai pushed my hand aside but headed for the door. "Let's walk, Nicholas."

CHAPTER NINE

I nto the cold night, we went.

Jai said nothing and I offered nothing. He was emotional but tried hard to restrain it, to maintain his composure. Reva's words had an impact, despite his wishes otherwise.

As for me, I meant what I said and was determined to listen.

Ginger had given me good practice—it helps you a great deal to learn to listen to everything unsaid when your companion can't speak.

Jai was saying so much, without a word.

The tenseness of his shoulders, the fast strides as he walked, the silent way he kept his lips tightly pursed. His mind was still locked from me, but the fear was evident.

Yes, fear.

I admit, I saw rage and disgust at first (there were still traces of it) but as we walked and the chatter of the others faded, true emotion began to emerge.

Fae might have been crafty, conniving even at times, and well known for their trickery but the art of outright lying was foreign to them. When the necessity of maintaining an air for the others was gone, the frightened Jai emerged.

I kept silent, intent on just maintaining the pace. Let Jai command the conversation.

How long we walked, I'm not sure but Jai finally came to a stop just before the three towering mountains that marked the most southern point. We called them the 'triplets' because they pressed into one another, like siblings leaning on each other.

"Do you know where we are, Nick?"

Honestly, I did not but that was not the answer Jai wanted. This place was important; it rang off Jai like bells. So, I didn't answer him immediately and began to pace.

Wide open place, shadowed by the mountains. Little in the way of trees but small shrubs and a pleasant enough stream that never quite froze completely.

I sat amid the snow, ignoring the frigid cold. Listen. Listen meant to listen to all. Use all the senses. My gloved hands dug into the white and my eyes closed.

Memory magic is an intriguing thing because it lives everywhere. The stronger the emotion, the stronger the magic. That's why I came to make a point—

No. Stop. Wait. Listen.

The howling wind, the slush of the snowy plains.

Yes...

It was here. Here was where I...

"I took my vow here." Standing, I brushed off my pants and faced Jai. "After you all took me and my wife in. It was here that I took my vow. That I would never leave, never expose you. You granted me leave to fulfill Christmas because I wanted it so. I thought...you did as well."

Jai pushed his long hair aside but it fell flat, as if weighed down with lead. "I did. For all my anger at humans, children committed no crime against us. At least not willingly."

I nodded. "And haven't I kept my vow?"

Eyeing me, Jai seemed to be...reluctant? His eyes scrunched and he turned away. "We hardly gave you a choice."

"What?" Indignation colored my words. "You set your rules. I agreed to follow them. Was it hard at times? Yes, of course it was! I wanted to see my family, to see my old hometown. When Noelle's father passed, when my sister passed...do you think we didn't stay up all hours, fretting over the fact we couldn't go to them?"

Jai looked back at me, and we finally locked eyes again.

"But I made you a promise, Jai. You and all the people here. I promised to hold to the rules of exile. I never broke it."

"You...didn't know?" The utter shock in Jai's voice. His hair fell flat and the light glow from his skin went dark.

"Know what?" I folded my arms. "I've been nothing but honest, Jai. I made a promise, I kept it."

"You...never tried to break your vow just because you made a promise?"

"Just?" Shaking my head, I said, "Jai, my friend, why give a promise if you have no intention of following it? Words are powerful, for good or bad. If I tell you I'm going to do something or not do something, I mean it." Huffing, both from the cold and the accusation, I said, "Did you think otherwise?"

"Everyone who takes a vow to join exile is magically bound." Jai took my hand and peered directly into my eyes. "If you had tried to break it, the magic of this place would have cast you down. But...you never even tried."

Well, forgive me for not knowing I was magically bound! "No one mentioned such a spell to me."

"So, I realize now. It was our way of reassurance. Of protecting ourselves. I thought for certain you must have known...but you didn't."

"No. Bit hurt by the prospect, to be frank. I made a vow. I keep it." It was hurtful, knowing my words had not been enough for him. I'd been locked here—though without my knowledge.

But could I cast blame on them for being so cautious? I was, after all, a mortal man at heart. Taking a breath, I softened my eyes. "I know humanity was cruel to your people, Jai. They've been cruel to one another for eons. But what they did to your people...undeserved."

I wish I'd had a better word but even with all the languages in the world, I lacked the vocabulary. "You should never have been made to hide up here. Not you, not the Doe Folk, not the dwarves. It isn't right. It never was right."

"Then, why do you ask us to break that exile?" The ferocity no longer dripped over his words. Sheer genuineness replaced it.

"Because. I see the greatness we could be together. I see the wonderful impact we could have on the world. As is, Christmas has become the season of joy. Of love. Of generosity."

"It is also a season of greed." Jai didn't interrupt me again, though.

"Yes, I will not deny greed will always be in the human race. It's not something, I think, we can fully eradicate. But that doesn't mean we shouldn't encourage those who carry charity in their hearts. It doesn't mean we shouldn't shun the children who have such big dreams." I eyed him. "As I recall, even you hold no grudge against children."

"No. I do not. The problem is that children grow up."

I frowned, my thoughts racing. His fears were solid, understandable. But how could I tell him, show him...

"Jai, I think things work in a circle."

He raised a brow at me, caught off guard. "A circle?"

"Yes. I believe the gifts failing, the magic of Christmas fading. It wasn't just one thing that caused that. It was many things. Magic, you once told me, is self-replicating. More comes the more it's used."

"Essentially yes."

"The children struggle with the idea of magic. With the idea of goodwill. I've seen it more and more these last few years. Didn't recognize it. Not fully. But I do now. Imagination no longer has the drive it once did. The world runs on metal, time restraints, efficiency."

I trailed off, quiet zapping my words. "Even we became poisoned by it."

Jai grasped my arm. "By necessity."

I shook my head. "It didn't need to be that way. But it happened. It doesn't have to stay this way."

Grabbing Jai by the shoulders, I leaned in. Almost forehead to forehead. "I blame my pup for making me see it."

"See what?"

"That you can't recognize something if you don't know what it is. I had forgotten about what listening...truly listening...was. And I'd forgotten what it felt like to be carefree, to be in the moment and enjoy what there was. No more, no less."

"And this pup showed you that?"

I laughed. A deep, belly laugh. "Her showing up kicked everything into motion. She showed me the flaws and led me to the answers. Reminded me of the simple magic of being young again."

Up and down, up and down, his judgement passed over me. "And?"

"And how are children supposed to believe in magic, in the belief of good providing the path, in miracles, if they never see them anymore?"

I looped my arm through Jai's, and when he didn't protest, began to walk.

"You and the others, you showed magic to children. Mystery. A spark of imagination. A promise that the impossible was possible. To think outside the box."

"Mankind has always had that ability." Jai reminded me. "Our presence doesn't create that."

"No, but remember that I said my little Ginger reminded me how to be carefree and again? How I had to be reminded how to listen again? How ALL of us are going to have to remember how to work with each other and not beside each other?"

Jai nodded.

"Well. It's easier to believe in something if you see it. It's easier to trust in something if you know it's true." I smiled. "It's easier to believe you can make a difference if you see others doing it."

Jai twisted his wrist and much how I had summoned images of the past, he did the same. Much more vibrant than I had managed to conjure.

But oh, the things I saw--inventions, medicine, architecture. The Renaissance itself. The literal art of science gaining traction.

But beyond that, through all the wisps of colors, I saw children being told stories. Hearing tales of mysterious miracles. Exploring woods no one dared venture to because the seed of curiosity was planted. The desire to innovate.

It all started from a story here, a kind gesture there. A glimpse of the impossible at the break of dawn.

And someone who believed them. Someone who told them: do it.

Jai dismissed it with a wave of his hand, sending fragments of color into the air. "I suppose believing in fairies and magic and miracles is easier with evidence of them."

"And look what children can grow up to be when they believe. I know it seems crazy but it's true. Children who change the world start by believing there's more than what they see. It's their own source of magic. And now...now, these children can learn about your people the right way. Not from stories to frighten them or old legends. From the source. From you."

Jai was silent, contemplating, the faint glow about him growing ever stronger.

"When you and Ginger stumbled upon me that night. I had felt...a change. A shift. In our magic. In my magic." He shuddered. "That's why I was out there. Trying, and failing to understand why it was changing."

Realization can come at once or gradually. For me, it always is both. In that moment, like the moment I realized I could put hope into the world and all barriers aside, I would, the answer came to me.

Simple. So simplistically complicated.

"It's circular. Curiosity. Imagination. Innovation. That's human magic. Maybe...we needed the magic of Fae, of elves, of all kinds. And you all, need us." I laughed, one full of relief and hope. "This entire world is a group project."

Oh, the face he gave. Shock, anger, astonishment, disbelief, and yet...amused pride. "We taught humans so well their own magic now dictates ours?"

"I dislike that term, Jai. It's more...grows. Nurtures. You all nurture mankind's imagination and our imagination nurtures..."

"Our magic." He scoffed, but not with malice. More like, amused astonishment. "A true symbiotic circle."

"In a world that's grown so much... distance, it's a dying breed of child, Jai." I gently touched him in the chest, where that magical core was pulsing with the urge to create. "But it's not gone. Not yet. To revive a dying fire, you still need a spark."

That awkward silence returned. Less than before but still the fear remained. What if I had not made my point? Speaking from the heart seemed the best approach. No lies, no falsities, just the reason Christmas meant so much to me.

I didn't share Jai or anyone's histories. I couldn't blame them for their fears, or their anger.But the things we could accomplish together. The things we could spark in those young hearts.

One didn't grow without stepping outside of comfort. We couldn't just linger.

Christmas couldn't die....

"Nicholas," he said finally. "Perhaps, I misjudged you. No. I know I misjudged you. When you first came here, I was so sure it spelled our doom. I nearly killed Sapir then and there. I should have known. The mountain accepted you. The spell—my spell at that, accepted you!"

"Something I still consider a great honor— "

"—But there's a magic in YOU, Nicholas. The things I've seen, the things I've survived, nothing should convince me to try this. But, listening to you...stars, I believe you. You bring hope, Nicholas."

What did you say to that? What *could* you say to that?

Thank you was hardly enough. Not even honored was appropriate. So, I smiled and said, "I think we find the people we're meant to meet."

"Tell the others to wait." Jai withdrew from our close circle. Away from me he went, in large strides, until the shadow of the mountain all but engulfed him.

It started small. A snowflake seemed larger, brighter. Some gained colors, some full of sound. Imagine rain where each drop was a tangible form of happiness.

It will not fully describe what I experienced but is the closest you will come.

It wasn't until Jai turned to me that realized—each light I saw was life. A spark of magic.

A voice.

Not voices like I was used to but a voice. Desire, fear, excitement. All contained in those fractals of color. Through all of it—trust and faith.

In me.

In Christmas.

"These...are all Fae voices," I said at last. "You called for more Fae."

"If we're going to know each and every child, if we're going to make each gift so unique that it lights that inner magic...we're going to need a lot of help."

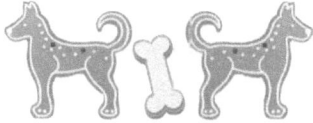

"The things I have missed, Noelle! I heard about them but oh, the stories were not enough!"

She laughed, for the third time, in the past fifteen minutes. The kind of laugh when someone dear to you has discovered something incredible and all you can do is relish in the joy on their face.

"What are they called again?" she asked, leaning against my shoulder.

"Hot dogs. With the works." I took another bite, dribbled more than a little on my shirt, and the remaining inch or so of the food plopped to the sidewalk.

Ginger quickly took care of it.

How long had it been since Noelle and I had walked among other humans? How long had it been since we'd known anything but cold?

It was one thing to see it, when going from house to house. One thing to hear about it in letters. But to walk it, observe grand buildings up close. To taste the food (hot dogs were like someone took my childhood favorites and them better) but most of all—to hear the children.

Oh, the laughter, the shouts, the cries as they played. It had been far too long. Even my strongest memories could not compare. No way to describe it beyond...my purpose had been born anew.

I fingered the small ring on my thumb.

Jai had spent days speaking with the other Fae he summoned. I was not privy to that conversation but whatever he'd said was heard.

They agreed.

The dwarves agreed.

The Doe Folk agreed.

Though, with caveats.

A haven was always needed—until it was determined it was not. So, while exile was not ended, it was no longer unending.

The North remained hidden, but so long as I—and by extension, anyone else serving the holiday—wore the rings, we could come and go as needed or desired.

Noelle and I were on our third excursion. To all who saw, we were an older couple with nothing quite extraordinary about us. An old man with a beard and a woman who walked a bit slow. And a small sausage dog.

So, we walked. We observed, we listened, with nary a sign we were doing so. A better method of seeing the true nature of children I had yet to find. Children showed so much of their true selves when they thought they were not being watched.

Or at the very least, not being watched by those they expected.

"How have the projects been going?" Noelle kept her voice down more out of habit than true need. "Is it true what I've heard? Of the successes?"

Eyes alight, I kissed her. "Oh, better than you've heard, Christmas Star. The latest I've heard is Sapir and Kaiya, with some help from Elder Gaian, had woven cloth from diamond and ruby. You've never seen the like."

Noelle adjusted her grip on Ginger's leash as the pup stopped, intent on rolling amid all the clovers. She'd all but pranced like a gazelle when she first saw grass.

"How are such rich cloths to be used?" Noelle smiled. "Not to make princess dresses?"

"Might have been before. But now...Alice who daydreams and draws and paints all manner of dresses of her own designs, can have her first attempt at making her own. With cloth she'll not find anywhere else."

"And that shimmers with the deepest gleam no matter how they are used. So, all she creates has a beauty no one else holds."

"And I can't wait to see what she creates. I can't wait until that young lad Samuel starts his own library."

I grinned and leaned close to her ear. "I cannot tell you how glad I am to have not just names but dreams on my list."

A quick squeeze to my side.

"Excuse us, 'cuse us!"

A sharp call, two voices, came from behind. Taking a step to the right, I pulled Noelle with me.

But Ginger was not about to move from her sanctuary in the green clover. Pulling the red leash from Noelle, I yanked on it but when she resisted, it pulled taut.

The first child coming behind us leapt over it. The second pitched forward and with their extra weight, the loop slipped from my hands.

Ginger took off for the small patch of wood like a shot.

"Ginger!" Noelle shouted, "Come back, girl!"

The two children, both girls, followed the last sign of the leash. The first ran after it without a word. The second turned to me and my wife.

"So sorry, Mister! Miss! We'll get her!"

With that, she was off like a shot, her blond ponytail flopping. I followed, Noelle on my heels.

Ginger was such a close-knit dog, why would she run? Pure curiosity and wanting to explore a world that was not made of ice, I suppose.

But what danger was here? So many things! She was so small, and for all her attitude, far more things were larger and more powerful than her...

"Ginger! Ginger!"

No reply, not even her enthusiastic barking whenever she thought she was clever. Was there a pond nearby? Could she have slipped into the water?

God, could she even swim? I know most animals can but what if she couldn't? I'd never been able to test it. Too cold up north!

The scenery became a blur. I searched, seeking that familiar ring of tan amid the green, the white, the—

"Oh, here she is, Mister!"

The second little girl's voice, and Noelle's arm on my shoulder, pulled me back to reality from the crazed miasma of panic that had swallowed me.

"See?"

As we emerged into a tiny clearing of clover and mushrooms, my errant dog was curled into the girl's arms, looking as if she had never committed even a thought of poor behavior in her life. Tail wagging and everything.

"Thank you," I knelt and scooped up Ginger, holding her tight. "She's a rambunctious thing, but that's not a bad thing."

Ginger looked up at me, dropped her ears partway, and whined.

"She's cute, Mister." The first girl spoke. "Sorry, we tripped over her leash."

Noelle chuckled. "No harm done. What were you running from?"

"Nothing, really. Just playing tag."

The boredom and dull emotion sank in my chest. An opportunity was here and I was loathe not to use it. "Oh, are you? Well, obviously my Ginger saw fit to lead you to something far more exciting."

"Exciting?" Both girls glanced around, no doubt wondering what excitement I saw that they didn't.

Pointing, I said, "Well, she led you to a fairy ring."

Truthfully, it was more fairy square but there were enough mushrooms for my purpose. Spark a thought, an idea.

"Fairies?" The first girl pouted. "Aren't fairies just in stories?"

Noelle smiled, "Oh, they might be. But I tend to think everything is "just in stories" until someone actually finds it."

A glint of color. Faint blue and green. A true blink of time.

Small but unmistakable. Some Fae were absolutely here. Not drawing a lot of attention but I suspect they caught wind of our situation and decided to have fun with it.

A spark of magic, just a brief hint something was there. Most people would have dismissed it or not seen it at all.

But both girls saw it though.

"What was that?" Both were suddenly knee-deep in the thicket, running their hands through the brush, each asking the other 'where was it, did you see it?'

Noelle and I stayed quiet, but Ginger nudged my arm and oh, if I didn't recognize that gleam in her eye. That knowing gaze.

She'd known. Whether she'd heard them, smelled them, or a combination of all of it, she'd tore her way in here.

"Look!"

A flash of blue light illuminated the tiny glen for a moment, coating everything in a cool hue. Amid the glow, I barely made out Una—in her diminutive form, finger to her lips in a teasing fashion.

She vanished as quickly as she came.

"Did you see- "

"It was a fairy! Wasn't it?"

"I didn't see wings..."

"But we're in a fairy ring!"

"It was hovering! She didn't need wings!"

Such a glorious thing to witness—when a spark becomes a flame. When the impossible becomes plausible. Because that marks the cascade of ideas, thoughts, and beliefs within a child's heart as they begin to tumble.

Hooking my wife's arm, we slowly departed, leaving two young girls to remember what it was to believe.

CHAPTER TEN

CHRISTMAS DAY, EARLY MORNING

Oh, what a sight to see as I exited the sleigh.

The village...was a village! Lights on everywhere! The lanterns were ablaze, tables set up with all manner of fixings. Small fire pits set up every few feet.

And amid them all—my friends. All the dwarves, the Fae, the Doe-Folk. Mingling, talking, sharing a drink, laughing. As if they had been friends for eons.

And we had, hadn't we? We'd just... lost sight of it.

"Merry Christmas!" I greeted as the sleigh touched down and I was on my way out before the last of my team had even fully stopped.

Two elves, along with three Doe-folk gently unlatched the reindeer, tossing heated blankets across their backs. I recognized Faluna bringing baskets of vegetables and fruits to their gathering.

As always, there was Noelle, arms wide open. I enveloped her, relishing in both the scent and the warmth. Planting a kiss on her lips, I said, "I think that is the best Christmas has gone in a long time."

"Did the new gifts go well?" Una approached, throwing a cloak around me. I grinned in answer as she squealed. "They did? The children love them?"

"We'll know for sure in a few minutes." Looking around, I laughed. "But look at this gift you've left me!"

Una smiled. "I can't take full credit. Everyone pitched in."

"Aye. There's plenty of salted meats, rich cheese, and fruity ale, my friend!" Sapir approached with a firm slap on my back. "It's high time we celebrated the right way."

"Together."

I turned and smiled as Jai made his way from the crowd. His hair pulled back with elaborate tinsel, he held Ginger close to his chest. "This little one was insistent on waiting for you all night. Noelle assured me that having her be our official food taster was a vital job."

"Oh, I'm sure she did brilliantly." Collecting the pup into my arms, she stood upright, using my elbow as a platform to plant several kisses on my cheek. "We have you to thank for all this, after all!"

"Do we?" Reva asked as she passed by, arms interlocked with Kaiya.

"Now that I think about it...yes." I smiled. "She snuck aboard my sleigh last year. She's the one who caught Jai's attention. That made me talk to Ieva...well Ginger was set on dragging me in there no matter what. That set my mind rushing."

"Then the visit with us," Sapir chimed in. "And didn't you run into the Doe Folk after you left?"

Looking down at my dog, I rubbed her neck. Leaning back, she rumbled, utterly content. "I was visiting the reindeer. Then this little one rushed off and well, it just spiraled from there."

"Wasn't it you who said we meet who were meant to meet?" Jai asked, something akin to joy on his face. At least as close as I had ever seen.

"And didn't I say that dogs choose their own people?" Noelle chuckled, and rubbed Ginger's head, "She got onto that sleigh for a reason."

I kissed the pup on the head. "The world weaves its own kind of magic, in so many different ways. Maybe the children knew we were at an impasse and needed a helper. So, they sent us a gingerbread pup."

A sharp bark, a pant then another kiss.

Making my way to the table, I indulged. Oh, the variety! Meats, cheeses, fruits, all manner of drinks (not all alcoholic), and more fresh bread and sweets than I believed could exist in one place.

But when I say the taste was astronomical, I mean it. Even my own Noelle's cooking, who as I've said, is always of the utmost quality, far exceeded even her most incredible past attempts. Rich, full of flavor, and bursting with tenderness, I don't know if anything will ever top what was served at those tables.

How could it? The memory magic was strong.

After a year of learning to work together, the side effect was we got to know each other. With that came the prospect of friendship, not just partnership. Where there was friendship, there was memory.

And where there was memory, there was magic.

So much of it I saw—a Doe Folk and a dwarf traded stories with Fae as an elf brought over another round of drinks. Without having to ask the preferences.

Fae lifted dwarves to add another touch to the silver bells on the tree.

Doe Folk raced elves for the desserts, slowing just enough for it to be close and promising 'You'll best me next time.'

Deep joy spread in my heart. Deeper than any ocean. Gratitude, appreciation, and oh, I-am-heard!

"The children!"

I don't know who proclaimed it first. I doubt it matters. All I knew was as I looked around, and it was as if magic itself came alive.

The lanterns around our courtyard burst into color—red, green, blue, and every other color. The warmth of not just a fireplace but a fireplace while draped in a blanket with a mug of hot cocoa flooded our square.

The Christmas tree sparkled with the light of a thousand stars, each one the brightest and most beautiful in the sky. The tinsel caught every color, cascading every face with a bright hue.

Brown crept its way into my Noelle's hair. My own beard grew less white and more tinted in silver. The aches in my joints softened.

Jai, who had stood by silently since bringing Ginger to me, closed his eyes. His straight black hair illuminated, taking more of an indigo shade and the tresses came alive, waving and billowing in the frosty night air.

When he opened his eyes again, they glistened, with joy reserved only for new life. As if he'd been born one more time.

"What is this?" he finally voiced. "I've felt all kinds of magic. Centuries of it, but nothing as poignant...as potent as this."

I had my suspicions; I'd felt inklings of it over the years. Always the best feeling. Warmth that defies description. Happiness without end. The feeling that despite all struggles, things will be all right.

Ginger nudged my chin, batted my nose, and gave a simple bark. The way she looked at me left no room for argument.

She knew. If I'd had any more doubts, they fled.

After all, Ginger was a pup that knew what she wanted. Knew what was needed.

"I think Ginger is right." Laying my hand on Jai's shoulder, I smiled. "Merry Christmas, Jai. This magic is the magic of hope."

"Hope," He repeated. "You humans put us all to shame."

"No," I corrected him, "This is what humans and Fae, humans and dwarves, humans and elves, and Doe-Folk...this is the magic we craft together."

"It's bottomless."

"And self-fulfilling. Hope feeds hope. We've lit the candle. The spark took."

He looked at me, at Ginger, at the glorious landscape around us. Reaching over, he caressed my pup's head.

"This is a grand magic, moreso than anything I ever thought myself capable of. If you will continue to serve us, little gingerbread pup, I will continue to learn it." Jai rose, grasped me tight by the arm.

Waving toward the others, Sapir, Kaiya, Noelle, Ieva, Kaluna and so many whose names I had yet to commit to memory, Jai drew us all together. A bundle, a hug, a collection of hearts.

"Together?" I asked.

"Together, Father Christmas."

ACKNOWLEDGMENTS

H appy holidays to all my wonderful readers!

Thank you so much for taking a chance with my little Christmas novella. It's my first foray into cozy fantasy after falling in love with the genre and it's been a truly enjoyable ride. If you enjoyed this story, please consider leaving a review. It truly helps more than you know!

This book is dedicated to an incredibly special pup---the Gingerbread Pup herself. While I chose to call her 'Ginger' for this story, she was very much a real dog. Her name was Ripley, and she was an utter joy to have in my life for 10 years. I hope that you have enjoyed meeting her through this tale.

For myself, one of the loveliest things I enjoy about the holiday season is the message of hope. It's a truly magnificent aspect and one that we need to continually feed. Sometimes, it's hard and sometimes, we need help to find ours again. The important thing is we keep re-lighting that spark.

May your holidays be full of hope and wonder and thank you all for being such wonderful readers.

Other Works Available by Cat Bowser

Fairy Stories Renaissance Series

MIRRORS AND ASHES—A SNOW WHITE RETELLING

THE SECOND STAR TRILOGY

Book 1: FINDING THE LOST BOYS